CATRINA

Elizabeth Daish

This first world edition published in Great Britain 1998 by
SEVERN HOUSE PUBLISHERS LTD of
9–15 High Street, Sutton, Surrey SM1 1DF.
This first world edition published in the U.S.A. 1998 by
SEVERN HOUSE PUBLISHERS INC of
595 Madison Avenue, New York, N.Y. 10022.

British Library Cataloguing in Publication Data

Daish, Elizabeth
        Catrina
        1. Love stories
        I. Title
        823.9'14 [F]

        ISBN 0-7278-2224-1

Typeset by Palimpsest Book Production Ltd,
Polmont, Stirlingshire, Scotland.
Printed and bound in Great Britain by
MPG Books Ltd, Bodmin, Cornwall.

CATRINA

Recent Titles by Elizabeth Daish from Severn House

EMMA'S WAR
EMMA'S PEACE
EMMA'S HAVEN
EMMA'S FAMILY
EMMA'S CHRISTMAS ROSE

AVENUE OF POPLARS
CATRINA
RYAN'S QUADRANGLE

One

Smooth silk fell apart as the hidden zip swung down past her hips and Catrina stepped out of the garment with practised careless ease that left the heap of silk uncrushed and ready for its hanger. She turned to the girl who stood holding the next in line of the bright clothes to be shown to the thoroughly satiated audience. The wealthy came to all the leading fashion gigs in case there was something that a rival might buy and wear to upstage them during the season, but even they could take in just so much and then they wanted other amusement.

Others, mostly buyers, watched the models and made notes when a particular new shape assaulted the attention, or a bright wig, more reminiscent of a Zulu warrior than a fashion model, erupted colour as the slender girl wearing it pranced the length of the catwalk and back, gyrating and posing and making the rippling flow of rich fabric mould to her limbs. A completely false impression of the shape of the confection was given to the often frankly plump ladies who marked their programmes and imagined themselves wearing something similar, adapted skilfully to their lack of inches in height and the excess of inches across the bum.

"Ready duckie? You're on next."

Catrina nodded, clutching at the feathers that had appeared on her head as if a conjurer had suddenly produced them from nowhere. She wriggled slightly to adjust the scarlet linen that encased her body. "They don't feel safe."

"Only as far as the end dais, then you throw them to the men on the right hand side," said the voice that patiently and relentlessly goaded her on to the long, dark-lined path among the dazzling, jerking lights and the canned music. "Take it slow and easy. No ballet. Make it sexy."

The hand twitched a seam and gave a gentle push. "Fantastic, darling."

To the cliché of 'Scarlet Woman', Catrina slid out into the lights and raised her head defiantly, pushing her shoulders into sharp peaks to make her boobs lie smooth and soft and gently swaying, while her hips tantalised the suddenly attentive men at the far end of the catwalk.

Briefly, she wondered who they were. Not the usual run of rival designers, the gossip hawks or fashion writers, and not husbands bullied into coming to watch the dresses, but who instead drooled at the girls, never noticing what they wore.

She turned, looked back and, completely dead-pan under the stark white make-up, stared hard at the three men at the side. Could be anyone; foreign businessmen sniffing at a good investment or visitors in the rag trade.

Now the turn as if she was walking away. Count one to ten and turn again and walk back towards them as if compelled to return. It was difficult to keep her lips from twitching. What reaction did Symfony expect? Usually the men who sat there would prefer a couple of butch gays to eye them from the rostrum or have the full attention of Louis, the second designer, more feminine than some of the girls on the ramp, but these men were showing all the right reactions. They were not any of Symfony's usual clients.

Crafty bitch, she reflected. Symfony knew they'd be there and knew that they'd react to a sultry approach, but why should I sell vicarious sex to three men in grey suits? I can't even see their faces clearly behind the lights.

She floated to the edge of the catwalk, swaying as if she might walk over it in a dream. Her green eyes flashed under the heavy make-up and her mouth was petulant. The men shifted uneasily on the small gilt chairs.

The feathers came away sweetly as she smoothed the lacquered fingernails over the wig to the pin holding them, and she scattered feathers of contempt and sheer sexuality over the men now openly wanting her.

Faces with holes for eyes stared up at her out of the twilight mist of dimmed lights. It was impossible to make out features, nor would she recognise them in a good light. There was just the shape of good shoulders and slim hips that filled the chairs and emanated more maleness than the elegant salon could use.

Now, turn and walk away with no backward glance. They must be forgotten and rejected like the feathers, but she wanted to turn, to peer through the shifting lights and blue twilight. Businessmen? Yes, almost certainly. Not a consortium of mafiosi. Symfony didn't have that hassle and Catrina had felt no threat apart from the blatant one of sex. She allowed herself a small smile as she reached the drapes and the dressers. At least the men didn't look like detectives or tax men, thank God. She'd have to do something about her tax returns.

"Great, fab and wonderful, darling." Symfony was purring. So she had seen the reaction, too. Did it mean a good order, a takeover, or just a personal triumph? They were obviously important. "DEE DEE! The white silk."

"But that's not until the end. I haven't another for ten minutes," Catrina protested. "You don't show the bride until last."

"Dee! Get a shift going, dear. No, don't call me that! We need Catrina in the white, now. I know, life's bloody hard. Now get it, you little cow." Catrina didn't even register the change from salon cream to Hackney Road, but Dee jumped to the change and Catrina was eased into the skin-tight sheath of irridescent white. "I know it's the virgin bit, but you don't wear a veil now. Leave the top five buttons open and put a bit more shadow between the tits."

"What now? Toss roses? You do know the make-up is all wrong? I was to have been cleaned up before this dress and have the dewy look. I'm like a ghost with all this white on my face and this wig."

"I'll die before this show is over," whispered Symfony. "One day everything will go on schedule and I'll be taken away by men in white coats! They have to go any minute now and they wanted to see you again. Dee, get some blusher to make her cheeks a bit more healthy."

"You can't! I'll look like a painted doll! This lot has to come off first."

"That's it! A painted doll. More red in sharp patches.

4

More lipstick. Fine. Tell Michael we want 'Living Doll' or he's for the chop! Now walk like an automaton, a zombie thing. Go down and look through them, not at them and come back. Just simply walk."

"I'm a model, not a nightclub come-on. I resent being used for bait."

"Yes, I know, we all do. Lovely. Now here comes Marcia. Has he got the music? Right! Off you go and then you can change. No bride for you today."

Feeling as if cut from cardboard, Catrina took long slow steps, her professionalism making her respond to the flow of the skirt, the lights and the throb of the hastily-found 'Living Doll'. This was an easy one, but she tensed as she came close to the men at the end of the walk. One had gone but the others stared up at her with interest and scarcely veiled lust. Remind me not to walk down dark alleys tonight if they are around, she thought, and wondered where the other man had gone, knowing that from him had come the laser beam of impact and that these two were mere voyeurs, fashion pimps on business.

Louis was waiting for her, looking puzzled and very miffed. "Lovely, duckie, but why the white without the veil? And those buttons!" He raised shocked eyebrows at the extent of the deep cleavage. The bridal dress was his idea and his mouth was tight with peevish annoyance.

"Not my idea, Louis. I only wear the rags." Catrina shrugged out of the dress, the chiffon face mask that protected the expensive fabric from make-up blurring her words. It had been a long session, very important for the salon for which she was working three shows but she knew that tempers had a habit of staying clamped down when big snags surfaced then breaking out over the stupidest trifles, usually at the end of a show.

"They seemed to like it," she said and smiled to make him relax. The thick white skin over her face dragged and she stopped smiling. "This white stuff will ruin my skin," she said. "If you ask me to wear it again, Louis, I'll have to get Max to ask for danger money." He winced and Symfony threw her a glance of gratitude. Anything to take his mind off the dress and his grievance, as the show had another five minutes to go and this was no time for Louis to throw a wobbly and louse it up.

"But you were to be the finale, in my creation," he said sulkily. "We pay you enough."

"The press took more pictures of this than they ever do of the bride," Symfony said. "The American buyers had to leave and wanted specially to see your dress, Louis."

Liar, Catrina thought. They wanted to see me, or two of them did. What happened to the other man who had been sitting back a little so that his face was even more indistinct than the others? He seemed different. Maybe he had a free seat and just took in part of the show to watch the girls. "They were very impressed," she told Louis and smiled again, forgetting her make-up. "Hell! I must get rid of this gunge on my face."

Louis preened. "We might keep the idea," he said, as if it was his own. "Living Doll has a good sound. I must make sure that the Duds and Drapes column got it right before they start guzzling our drinks and forgetting why we invited them."

Catrina sat by the mirror, cleansed her face and throat and took a deep breath. It was a relief to let her own fine skin emerge and to see that it was none the worse for its burial. She wiped away every trace and sat drinking mineral water with ice, tired beyond imagining, or rather oddly depressed in a way she couldn't recall happening after such a well-organised and stimulating show.

The ripples of admiration greeting her entrances still gave her a thrill of achievement after two years as a recognised top model, earning a fantastic income and being feted wherever she went. This show had been no different except for the one sudden change in the programme. Even that had been slight. The dress was the same, the only thing that was not so was the ambiance and the projection, from a veil and the dewy-eyed anticipation of marriage to the hard white heat of offered passion that was used to further the prosperity of the salon.

Don't be stupid, she told herself. It's all sex. Why should it depress me today? Just because I couldn't walk on looking like a sex starved kitten? Who in this place watching believed in that crap anymore?

The girl came to shampoo her hair and brushed it first into long shining fair swathes. The delicate scent of the conditioner filled the dressing room and bathroom and let Catrina forget the aura of stale perfume and sweat in the changing rooms. She showered, washing away tension and let the soft shower gel flow smoothly over her shoulders and body, then dried under a thick towelling robe while her hair was arranged.

Catrina examined her toes and wondered if she needed a pedicure. The pictures for *Summer Vogue* would have to be done soon, meaning bare feet and sandals and beach wear. A flurry of sleet on the glass roof made her shiver. Why do I carry on with this work? The money, of course, and the admiration. How could anyone pose in mid-winter and smile, ignoring icy winds and black skies, pretending to bask in summer heat, unless they were mad or well paid?

Not always well paid. It was ironic that she had endured all that when she was less well known, putting up with bad hotels, cold water in the taps and warmed only by the dream that one day she would appear on the covers of the leading glossies and be given homage for her beauty. She had paid far too much for studio portraits for her folder when she could ill afford it and now they paid her for everything, as Max, her agent, screwed the last penny out of each deal.

She could afford the best, but now the best was thrust on her as her due and a dinner costing more than she once earned in a week was often urged on her as if her presence in the restaurant did them a favour. Even the settings were good now. No draughty Bognor Beach, hiding behind wind shields to do her hair and hoping that goosepimples didn't show on film, but Bermuda, Mustique and Cannes made light of the weather.

The water in the cut glass beaker was cold and she sipped it with pleasure. Fashion shows in the provinces were never like this and now she had time to relax and compose herself for whatever function Max had lined up for her tonight. She giggled and the sound was oddly innocent, bouncing back from the black and gilt walls. Suppose I don't go? Suppose I go out and buy a hamburger and opt out of the supper party? He'd kill me! She glanced at the invitation stuck on the mirror. At least one member of parliament and a leading heart surgeon were dying to meet her.

She wrinkled her nose, aware that it was now possible to do so without feeling that the skin would crack. She looked at the rail behind her. Symfony was a very practical woman. It might seem unnecessarily profligate to sling an expensive creation into the lap of an already highly paid model, as if she was glad to be rid of something fit only for a jumble sale, but it made good sense. Symfony knew that before the supper party on a boat moored by Victoria Bridge, there would be a photographic session under the chandeliers of a famous club in St James's and the pictures, when seen in every capital in the world, would bring orders flooding in to her salon. It was wonderful free publicity.

"Come in," said Catrina.

Symfony flicked her tongue over dry lipstick and grinned when Catrina handed her a beaker of iced mineral water. "Ta," she said. "I could get to like this. Did you ever feel so dry?"

"But worth it? I thought it went well."

"Fantastic, darling. You were out of this world. The men at the end were nearly up there with you!"

"Better raise the catwalk. I could feel the angst from where I was. Who are they?" She smoothed moisturiser onto her face and throat.

"A new firm. One was with Crinkles of Boston but he set up alone and now is scouting for stock."

"All of them?"

"Two. The other one was there to see you."

"Me? As a person? Have I met him? It's infuriating.

From the top I can never see them clearly through the lights. I saw three men and then only two at the end. Did he get tired of watching or decide that he had lost interest in me?"

"They all want to meet you, duckie, but I told them you had to be at St James's and then on to the reception on the Thames and you wouldn't have time."

"You didn't ask me!"

Symfony shrugged. "You should be grateful. We block all the casuals and the nutters and give Max details of the others. If they are valuable, he'll fix a meeting."

"Does everyone have to be . . . of use to me? I'm a big girl now, Symfony. I have always been free to choose the men I meet and I can lose the ones who are too pressing or boring." She recalled that every man she had dated during the past year had been carefully chosen and presented to her as if they had been washed and sorted before she saw them. All were rich, intelligent and well educated but most had been boring or intent on showing her off like some rare orchid.

She smiled. The exception had been the rock singer who had homed in by her side at a charity show, but when they met after the show they had shared a mutual consternation. He was exactly as he was on stage, with psychedelic clothes and kitchen cut hair, while she had slipped into something muted and elegant, with little make-up and an air of amused innocence. They had laughed, vowed they had pressing engagements elsewhere and had not met since, so perhaps Symfony had a point.

"You'll use the new Orchid Look?" Symfony eyed the pots of cream on the dressing table with some anxiety.

"You've already fixed it, haven't you? All for free?" Catrina mocked her gently.

"You keep the dress," Symfony said quickly. "Wear it and the new make-up and a dab of this." She held up a flask of scent that was expensive enough to be the original holy ointment but a hundred times more fragrant.

Catrina put some on the pulse at her wrist and in the bend of her arm. "Ummm, yes, I like it. Do I keep this?"

Symfony hesitated, then nodded and Catrina knew that she had another favour to ask. "Of course you keep it. You've earned it," she said and smiled. "You are the best."

"I've earned it? Does that mean I don't have to do anything more than I've done today except to pose in your creation, poncing about to show the label if possible, wearing make-up created for your next show and the perfume you were promised by the makers if you could persuade me to wear it? What do they want you to do? Give away five drops in tiny phials at the show on Sunday? What if I want to go out in jeans tonight with bare skin and a nice healthy soap smell? Meet a student I once knew and share a bottle of gin?"

"You'd hate all that now," Symfony said calmly. "Louis is over the moon and keeps trying to tell me about this wonderful idea he's had about dressing girls as dolls." They exchanged amused glances. "You aren't with us at the show in Surrey tomorrow, and I can't ask you to put that stuff on your skin again but I can get one of the girls to put it on and the punters will never know who is under the plaster."

11

"I did ring Max. Has he been in touch? I pointed out that if he lined me up for that kind of gig, he'd have to get my skin insured before taking any more liberties with it."

"So he said, but we do seem to have a nice gimmick here. We've been ringing round to find a ventriloquist act to set the scene and been round the agents for a talking doll. You know, a big one, almost human. Louis is even now making a huge rag doll to sit by the microphone."

"And the ethnic bits that haven't gone so well this year might fit the scene? Nice thinking. I almost wish I was working with you, but I'm going down to my old home to an aunt I haven't seen for far too long. It's over the hill from the stately home where you will be. If she's interested, I may bring her along to watch. It could be fun to see you all from the other side of the lights."

"Great. Can I quote you'll be there?"

"No press," Catrina said firmly. "Give the locals a break as I don't know if we'll make it. It's my day off and I'm not posing in a draughty garden for free."

"Right. Maybe just as well if your old auntie dislikes reporters camping near her gate to get the lowdown on what Catrina was really like as a baby."

"Not so old, more like an older sister but nice. I write to her twice a year, send her cards from some of the locations and buy her exotic shawls and carved figures that she'll never use. I also send her invitations to smart functions but she never has the courage to go. Tomorrow, I'm strictly incog and Carol must come first. If a local photographer spots me, then it'll make his day, if not his fortune."

"Fair enough. Just be beautiful for us on Sunday for the

charity show. Lord Justine made it clear that unless you walk down that ramp he isn't willing to lend his historic mansion for the function after the dress show."

"Old goat," said Catrina mildly. "But the exercise will do him good trying to run me to earth." She sat side saddle on her stool. "Tally-ho!"

The door opened and Louis staggered in, his face red with effort and a huge limp doll slipping from his arms. "Isn't she marvellous? I want one of the bitty skirts; you know, the Cinderella look. All uneven hems." He pulled the high-necked shirt down and pinned it at the waist to keep the neckline low and Symfony ran, knowing that this would be one of Louis's brighter efforts, and a little service made him brilliant. Fascinated, Catrina watched the doll completed, from the punk hair-do down to the shiny, black, patent-leather pumps on the slim, life-like feet. She giggled as the doll flopped over the man's shoulder when he tried to sit it up straight. She was reminded of an inflatable doll whose function was better not imagined and in any case would have no relevance to Louis.

"It's almost human," Symfony said. "Is one going to be enough?"

"I've thought it out. The girls in the work room are sewing the mark two version but I wanted to see one finished. They'll be exactly the same down to the shoes. We found that these pumps were easy to slip over the feet and they have no heels to catch in things. I think they look more raggetty doll, too." He beamed and sat back on his heels. "I can see it, can't you, Sym? We'll have pale green lights for the opening and then the vent act."

"Not too long or they'll think they've come to a Punch and Judy and not a fashion show," Symfony said.

"Yeah. Not too much. There'll be one doll on either side and two of the girls sitting with them, looking just like them. Music, and the girls get up slowly and move down the walk."

"If the dolls stay there all the time, why not change the angle of the lights from time to time? It gives an illusion of movement," Sym suggested.

"You're so right, Sym." He hugged her. "This is going to be good."

"What about the ventriloquist? They aren't found on every street corner."

"Pat gave me the idea," he said. "She mentioned that there was one staying at the hotel where she hangs out and said she feels a bit sorry for him as his bookings are down, so he's easy to get. He has a life-sized doll too which makes it simple. We can dress her like the others and he'll have to dress the part, too."

"Not too much gypsy theme. Much too twee," Symfony said. "He'll have a DJ. They all do as part of the equipment and that will be fine. Does he know the venue? Maybe if Pat knows him she can bring him there."

Catrina frowned. "The pretty girl with dark hair and eyes? I haven't really spoken to her but I heard that she had been living with a man in showbusiness. Could that be the one? Maybe they got back together but I heard that she was on her own now, and he'd gone to Ireland."

"She was anxious for the man to get this job and said he was a Cypriot trying to get known in Britain, but it sounded as if she was just sorry for him and had no ties there."

"She might have got to know him when we did that commercial on Cyprus wines," said Catrina. "The locals loved watching and taking part. I can place her now as the girl in the red skirt with the lemon blossom. Max said that she had something special and looked a bit pensive when he saw the stills. He's either going to take her on his books or try to make her. You know Max." She laughed. "If you've quite finished covering me with ends of cotton, you can get out and leave me in peace. I have to be ready for Max in half an hour. See you at the reception?"

"Not me," said Louis. "I have to get this right and choose clothes for the two living dolls . . . living dolls . . . good, ha?" He propped the doll against the table. "I'll leave this one here for now," he said.

Symfony's eyebrows shot up. She shrugged. "Great, Louis," she said.

Catrina finished her make-up. The dress was a honey, with all the muted elegance that made Symfony's salon so famous among the seriously rich. She had chosen this dress well, with none of the quirkiness of the more way out models of the afternoon, and had made no attempt to jazz up the image of her favourite model. Carefully, Catrina viewed herself from all angles in the triple mirrors and was satisfied. She was still pouting into the mirror, unsure of the lipstick, when a tap on the door made her say "Come in," before she had time to wonder who it was.

"What the hell is that?" Max stopped short and stared at the finished doll sitting drunkenly on the floor. "A bit old for dolls, aren't you? Or is it a gift from a friendly madman?"

"One of Sym's brainstorms. Must be good as Louis pinched the idea as his and is even now making another just like it."

"Christ, he could buy one!" Max grinned. "Perhaps not our Louis. I saw the reflection in the mirror as I came in and it made me feel quite peculiar. Must it look like that?" He sat the doll straighter. "That's better. Looks less . . . less . . . well, better."

"Less dead," said Catrina. "I feel that I want to close those dark staring eyes. I couldn't live with it in my room, could you?"

"You don't have to. The evening is all set, and I have a cab waiting. You look divine. Do you keep the dress?" She nodded and held out the bottle of scent. "And that? It cost a bomb." Max smiled at the doll. "Well, lady, we'll say goodnight. Don't frighten the cleaners when they come. Here, have a dab of this to cheer you up." He took the glass stopper and put scent on the back of the doll's neck. "No ears so that's the best I can do."

He switched off the lights and Catrina locked the door and handed the key to the porter on the ground floor. She put her gloves in her pocket and followed Max to the taxi. He carried the small case that she took with her on every assignment and Catrina reflected that assignments and free time merged in a frightening way, leaving her no time to think, to laze, to visit a club of her own choosing, to play badminton or go swimming or to visit old friends.

"What now?" she asked and nodded as he read out a list of names who would be at the reception and who might be useful contacts. She sighed. "Tomorrow, I shall lie in until nine, have whatever I fancy for breakfast, and swan off to Surrey for a whole day. I can bear to work tonight if I can have that break."

"Sweetie," began Max.

"Not one single word, Max! I know what's coming. You just happen to have a tiny job that I ought to do tomorrow. It's not much but I shall be seen and the press will be there. No dice! I haven't had a break for weeks and I'm going down to Surrey."

"Be reasonable."

"I spend my life being reasonable. I work so hard that I don't know if it's night or day half the time, and I shall look like a hag if I don't get more sleep."

"You, a hag? Have you seen the latest pictures for the American magazine? They are superb. Now, about tomorrow."

"No, Max. If the world comes to an end, sorry. I'm having a day off and pleasing myself. Just one day."

"It isn't a job. It's an old friend of yours over from the States. He wants to see you."

"How old and how much of a friend? Not Gabry? We're through for good."

"No, not him. This one is from way back, or so he says. No, don't look like that. I promise he's not another Hooray Henry wanting to make you. I remembered a bit of what you said about your home town. He knew where you were brought up and seems kosher. Knew your family and the school."

"That's nothing. After the last interview, everyone in London could say that about me. If he's genuine he must stay on ice as I have work to do." She looked out at the lights of the West End and gathered her coat around her, as they slowed down before the glowing entrance of the club in St James's. "I have nobody left of my family except for my aunt Carol who is more like a sister than an aunt, and no sentimental hang-ups for spotty boys I met at school." She set her shoulders. "Smile, Catty, you're on camera," she said.

As soon as the car released her, she stood tall on the pavement and smiled, giving her best, patiently turning from side to side for two full minutes, then walked briskly to the doorway, turned for one last smile, giving the photographers plenty of time. It kept her image good with the press and she sympathised with anyone waiting in the cold.

Three years ago it might have been her, travelling by tube and waiting for autographs if she had been interested in any of the celebrities, but now, she was the one to see faces turned to her, smiling hopefully. She signed at least two dozen cards, envelopes or notebooks and only then followed Max, who was quietly fuming at the delay.

"There's no need," he said.

"I was a pedestrian once and now I can drive. I remember the cold."

"You been at the mineral water again?" he asked in mock alarm. "You're as nutty as they come. Get in there and make an impact on the ones who count."

"I already have," she said and slipped away to the cloakroom. Two minutes later, she was with him, smiling and bright with the glow of perfect everything. Only her eyes were over-bright as one after another they came to talk and to admire and to want her as men want an expensive plaything, women want to copy and to envy and the Press want to take and exploit.

A glass of champagne urged on her was sipped and then held lightly, hardly making the level of the bubbles less. Too much of too many delicious foods was offered and rejected, with a special smile for the hard-working waiters. Everyone felt that they had something from her and none managed to chip away the bright shell of perfection to glimpse what might be beneath.

"Doing fine," whispered Max. "Now, about tomorrow."

"Tomorrow, I don't exist. I am not available."

She smiled again as Symfony came towards her in a weird but strangely beautiful caftan. The last photograph was in the can and there was only the reception to face. A car and another foyer, more waiters with more champagne and food and bright lights burning into her eyes.

In ten years, what then? she wondered. Without enough sleep, the growing constant dread of dying beauty would bring emptiness to the eyes now adoring her, so what should she do? Marry one of the men who offered money, position and titles or ranches in Texas? Life in the West or in some crumbling castle, with smelly dogs and inarticulate homage? Children or the need to keep her figure? Endless talk of fashion or could there ever be a lover who didn't care about the shade of her lipstick or knew nothing about the perfect set of a gown?

She took a tiny asparagus roll and a sip of champagne. I'm getting lightheaded without food, she decided, and these bubbles give me headaches. Behind her eyes was a dark cloud of growing depression as she smiled again and again.

Symfony came over. "You aren't eating. Don't get high on nothing. Can you bear just one more intro?" Catrina shook her head and Sym looked as if she cared and understood. "You've had enough, duckie. Scrub that one. Don't want you falling apart, do we? Forget it. I'll tell him you've left."

"Thanks, Sym. Do that. I am leaving now. Can someone get me a cab?" She collected her coat and made a face at Max, who was waving to catch her attention from the doorway to the reception, urging her to come back. She turned away, not ready to look tired but feeling it creeping up. The outer door on the deck of the moored boat opened readily to her hand and the night air of the city was cool and damp. A car drew up and she bent to ask if it was for her.

"Hello, Catty," said the man behind the wheel. "Can I drop you off?"

Two

"MAX!"
He heard her and turned sharply. "I thought you'd left. Anything wrong?" He took her hand in his and found it cold. "Let's get out of this before anyone sees you."

"I was leaving and a car tried to pick me up outside. I can't explain it but I was suddenly very scared."

"You told him to sod off?" Max put a comforting arm round her shoulders. "You're tired, sweetie. Only the usual kerb crawler along the Embankment, hoping for something superior." His shrewd eyes narrowed. She was really upset as he had seldom seen her. The bright smiles were so much a part of her that he no longer knew when it was for real, and now that facade was weakening as he watched her sink into a chair by the exit. "I'll take you home and look under the bed for bogeymen," he said, and spoke to a porter who looked out of place dressed like a Victorian sailor. Two minutes later they were walking out again over the red carpeted gangway from the glittering boat that had never looked so smart in all its years at sea.

Catrina glanced across at the line of cars parked on the

other side of the wide road and wondered which it was. In the damp river mist they all looked alike, the colours absorbed and cancelled by the night. Max was right. The man who had called her by the name she hadn't heard for so long must have read an account of her life in one of the womens' mags and latched on to her pet name. Everyone who had ever heard of Catrina must by now know that she had been called Catty at school.

At the time of the interview, she had said too much, giving away what seemed at the time innocent and amusing things about her childhood. They'd even wanted a picture of her in a cat suit with furry ears, a bit over-done, but she had treated it as a joke, and now she wasn't sure. Slowly and inexorably, her whole life and personality were no longer hers and she had a growing sense of panic that she might never catch up with her own publicity and regain her identity.

"Better now?" Max glanced at his watch.

"Sorry, Max, I had a sudden low and wasn't up to my usual strength. He might even have known me but I don't think he was Press; so one less man at my feet." She smiled weakly. "Stay and have coffee?"

"No, I'll just pop you inside and make sure everything is all right and you won't have the creeps, then I must go."

"You've a date? Oh Max, I'm sorry."

"No rush. You gave me the excuse I needed to leave early. Dudley wanted to make up a poker game and I needed a discreet excuse, so when he saw me leave with you he backed off as he respects the fact that we must have business to discuss."

"He doesn't think you're here for the night?" She

giggled. "That's one they haven't pinned on you yet."
She felt better. Max had strength and was a friend as
well as her agent, but was notorious for one night stands
with some of the girls on his books and those he met at
shows. Catrina was amused at his success. "Is she worth
the wait? Tell her that I went all hysterical because you
don't love me any more."

He grinned. "You couldn't say that to just anyone.
You are damn lucky to have me as an agent. I never
mix business with pleasure, at least not regular business
like ours."

He unlocked the outer door to her apartment and
switched on the lights. A warm glow of pastel lighting
swept the sitting room and brought the white leather and
suede upholstery into gentle relief. Max walked swiftly
into the bedroom and more lights came on, reflecting the
coffee sheen of the silk bedcover and the thick white rugs.
Glass bottles and jars glittered along the wide dressing
table, holding the secrets of perfect make-up, efficient
disguise and a contribution to fame.

Catrina watched him. "All clear," he said. "Not even
a tax man lurking in the bathroom or looking at your
books in the study. Which reminds me. I have a very
good man coming to sort out your tax. He'll be in touch
next week."

"You're a pal, Max." She touched his hand. "You can
go now. Tell her she's a lucky girl and don't ditch her
too soon. It's time you settled down."

"I know, but I enjoy browsing. You can talk! When do
we see you drifting down the aisle at St Margaret's in one
of Louis's less freaky gowns?"

"I told him NO."

"There goes your insurance. Nice little pad he has in Scotland, bijou palace in Mayfair and a few properties scattered over the hot spots of the world."

"He looks fine as he takes after his mother, but have you seen the ancestral portraits? I can't risk my children having the family chin and those pale boggling eyes."

"You have a point. See you. Have a good day tomorrow."

Catrina went to the window to watch him leave and smiled as she recalled that he'd made no further reference to work tomorrow. Even Max had a heart. She looked down into the quiet street. It was raining softly and there was no wind. From the city came the muted whisper of night cabs on wet roads and the faint moan of a boat on the river. She dropped the edge of the curtain, and then peeped again as a car drove slowly past the block of apartments. She glanced at her watch. At three in the morning, traffic either went by in a hurry, stopped firmly to disgorge passengers or parked for the night.

The car came back on the near side, paused as if the driver wanted to set the address firmly in his mind and accelerated in the direction that Max had taken in the taxi that had ticked while he saw Catrina safely home. She closed the drapes firmly. I'm getting neurotic, she decided. I am harrassed by one driver and another just got lost and had to find his bearings. London is full of cars and if I don't get to sleep I'll never make Surrey tomorrow.

Long discipline made her cleanse her face but she was too tired for more. A hot drink of milk and chocolate made her feel small and indulged. Catty, she thought. Hot chocolate and biscuits and Surrey tomorrow added up to a retreat to childhood. Her hair spread over the pillow and she slept like the child she had been, had lost and mourned in the birth of Catrina, the woman who needed no second name.

The lights were on when she woke to the alarm call she had forgotten to cancel. "Christ! I don't have to get up yet!" It was seven o'clock and she had no need to leave before nine. Coffee and toast filled the apartment with a fragrance that made her feel hungry. She had eaten nothing for hours before the hot chocolate so she made an extra slice of toast and sipped orange juice while she opened her mail. Two invitations made her raise her eyebrows. Max could answer them. A few pleas for her to open charity functions; Max could deal with them, too. Letters from friends she had seen some time ago made her feel guilty that she wrote so seldom and the junk adverts went into the waste bin.

An offer of a ridiculous sum for a few minutes nude photography made her smile. Max was almost prudish when it came to her baring her body, and even the top designers knew better than to expose too much of the divine form. He would tell this lot exactly where to go! She remembered her reaction to the first of these offers, thinking that even if it was not really her scene it was money for nothing. "Never, ever do it," he'd said firmly. "It pays and everyone does it, maybe. When they do, they lose something. Even Monroe suffered from those early poses."

Nudity. She stretched and yawned. It would be good to sleep in the raw with someone who really loved her. She turned on the shower. That way lay nostalgia and unhappiness. She patted body lotion over her breasts and cradled their fullness in her hands. Later she would think of love and maybe marriage or a stable relationship. She smiled sadly. Six months ago she'd said the same and still the wheel turned full circle from show to show, to commercial to public appearance and back to the empty apartment when she had time to spare.

She reached over for the phone. "Hello," she said.

"Symfony here. I didn't ring earlier as I knew you'd be asleep." Catrina glanced at the clock. It was still only seven-thirty. "I'm in a bit of a spot. Patricia hasn't turned up for rehearsal and doesn't answer the phone and we leave for Surrey at eleven."

"And?" Her voice was sharp.

"I know you have an aged aunt or someone to meet." Symfony dismissed Carol without a sigh. "Bad luck on her of course but there will be other days. We'll double your fee. We've heard that the Americans want to be there and they want to see you."

"So Pat hasn't gone sick? That's just an excuse? Sorry, Sym, I'm on my way to my aged aunt to feed her breakfast, the poor old soul!"

"Wait . . . Pat really hasn't turned up, that's for real."

"Ring the agency. There must be lots of girls all panting to appear in one of your shows. If you put all that goo on their faces, what does it matter who is under it? I can't come to work but as I said last night I might trundle my poor old aunt along in her wheelchair if she feels up to it."

"There is another thing."

"I thought so. The other sounded thin."

"The man you couldn't see last night is very anxious to meet you. He asked me to contact you and say that Paul had called."

"Paul who?"

"He said he knew you at school and after, but he's been out of the country for a few years."

"So he expects to see the same spotty girl he remembers? Most of the boys I knew there I wouldn't touch with a ten foot pole."

"He was at the show but was fooled by the white make-up and couldn't believe that it was you."

"So he saw my picture in one of the glossies and thought he'd drag up a past acquaintance? Surely you didn't fall for that old trick? I take it he's in the business and thinks he might ask me to do some work for him for old times' sake?"

"He's in manufacturing for the rag trade in the States and Canada." Symfony named the firm and Catrina couldn't help being impressed. "I'm sure it isn't the usual come-on, duckie. I gave him your address."

"You what?" Catrina grabbed the receiver before it hit the floor. "You know you never, never do that!"

"I'm sorry, dear, I didn't think you'd mind. Lovely voice, and nice eyes. Not your actual smoothie."

"You sound as smug as a fat cat. What's he promised? A good order for the chain store side of his business? Adaptations from your models?"

"Business is business," Symfony said complacently, "and this one is different."

"What makes you so sure?"

"He knows one of your relatives, a Carol something?"

"He does? Now isn't that strange, I can ask her if she does know him. I'm seeing her today."

"I know that and so does he now. I just had to explain a little as you were so elusive." The voice was placatory. "He's nice, really he is. He does know you from way back and if you hadn't run away like a scared lemming last night, he could have put you in the picture."

"He said that?"

"What?"

"The scared lemming bit."

"I suppose so. Something like that. He was trying to give you a lift from the boat but you shied away and left at the speed of light." Symfony was amused. "Not like you, duckie. I've known you to tell them to drop dead in five languages."

"Lemming . . . he said that? I haven't heard that for a very long time, Sym. Now I'm telling you to get lost, in good plain English! I go to Surrey and maybe, just maybe, I'll take in the show as a spectator. Get a girl from the agency or paint your own face white!" She ignored the pathetic bleat. "Goodbye, Sym," she said, and put the set down on the table.

She sat with her legs tucked under her on a round, deep, womb-like cushion, staring at the phone. When it rang, she put out a hand and smiled. "Hello, Paul," she said.

"Hello, Catrina?" The voice was slow, with the right

degree of caution for one who had not been in touch for five years. "It *is* Catrina?"

"I am she," she said formally. "How did you find me?"

"I just opened a magazine, any glossy magazine, and there you were."

"I do get around," she agreed. The voice was his, if a little deeper and somehow more serious. The Paul she remembered had a light, carefree, throwaway style that was fun, but she sensed that he had matured. He might even be stuffy. She damped down her pleasure. "I'm sorry I didn't meet you last night, but it isn't exactly wise to accost women alone on the Embankment in the early hours of the morning as if you were a common kerb crawler."

"I'm sorry about that. I could have kicked myself as soon as I saw you back off. I do apologise."

Oh dear, he was closing up instead of getting the formalities over in a flood of shared reminiscences.

"It was good of you to phone. I hate loose ends and did wonder who you were. I'm going out now, so you must excuse me as I have to get ready." It gave him a let-out. All he had to do was to make polite noises and put down the phone and everything would be as if he had never tried to contact her again. Her hand tightened on the white plastic. "It would be good to go over old times," she added politely. "But we are both very busy people."

"That's why I thought I could save you some time today and let you relax." The relief was there now. He's saying what he wanted to say but couldn't spit out. He's doing *me* a favour.

"Oh?" was all she could say but she was strangely pleased and knew that she was smiling.

"I can pick you up at nine-thirty and take you down to Carol. It's on my way. I have to be at a fashion show this afternoon and Carol said she'd give me lunch first and we can all talk. She knows that you don't enjoy driving."

"I drive very well."

"That isn't the same. You always liked . . . but times change."

"I'll be ready." The clothes chosen for the day were all wrong. She lifted an armful of skirts onto the bed with the day dresses such as she'd worn to the castle in Scotland. If she went to the show, even as a spectator, she would be expected to look good. She chose a silk suit of pale green and slung a gold, satin-lined coat over her shoulders. The soft bag with make-up and some high-heeled sandals were enough with the slip of a dress if she went out to dinner, and the coat was reversable.

She checked her purse for bankers cards and cash, and as the doorbell rang, she was staring at an old photograph of school children on a picnic. Hastily, she put it in a drawer. He'd think her an idiot if he knew she had kept it all this time. It was Carol who formed the links with the past, not the past itself, so full of light laughter and then anger.

He stood in the doorway and looked past her at the opulence chosen by a famous interior designer. He was smiling, with a twitch to his lips that meant, who would have thought it possible? She had an absurd desire to push him away from the door and shut away the room, pretending that it didn't belong to her but was only on loan. "Hello," he said.

"Paul? I hardly recognised you."

"You aren't exactly the same either." He looked at her with a smile of formal greeting. His handshake was firm and noncommittal and the tiny flame died. He had changed. How could she expect him to be the same after all this time and after everything that must have happened to him? How could she expect to see the Paul who swam with her, played tennis with one string broken in his old racquet and who could beat everyone in the school at conkers? And later, that thin boy had danced with her, taken her on the back of his black motorcycle, with her arms clinging to his wiry hips and the smell of oil permeating her clothes long after she was home again.

"It's good of you to bother," she said. "Carol will be pleased to see you. I had no idea that you two kept in touch." How could I know when I told her that I wanted to hear nothing about you or where you were? How could I know, when I was the first to leave to make the bright lights and to laugh at settling down?

Time had killed the memory of that haunted young face and then his defensive anger, sharp and insulting. Memory dimmed the injustice of his arrogance, his sneering taunts that fame was only possible for her through the casting couch or its equivalent.

"Is that all you are taking?"

"One key, one small bag and a purse," she said. "I learned to travel light and I have clothes at Carol's suitable for the country." He must have lost his virginity too. Should I resent that or be glad that I didn't cloud his life? "Quite ready," she said.

"Fine. I parked along the road. It's stopped raining so you won't get wet and it isn't far." He didn't touch her as she stepped out on to the shining sidewalk and the lack of contact was poignant. Once, long ago, he would have taken her hand and swung it as they walked. But that was two other people, centuries ago. Once, even if it looked heavy, he would have strode ahead, ignoring the fact that she carried a case, but now he carried the small designer square of baggage but managed not to touch her hand when he took it from her. Why hadn't she noticed last night that the car had an American drive?

"Nice car. Did you bring it over with you?"

"Yes, I like it and I thought it might be useful."

It was expensive; much more expensive than it looked at first glance, as most good things are. "Wouldn't it be more economical to hire while you're over here?" Now he'd have to say if he thought of staying. She smiled. "I'm money conscious just now. My accountant gave me a rocket last week for carelessness and told me to keep all my receipts. Cars, I gather, cost money."

"He's right, and you are about the hiring, but I plan to be here for a while and I like to carry my home with me."

She looked at the long low lines that could take a lot. "You don't live in it?" It was possible. He never did like being cluttered.

"Not exactly, but I can telephone and fax from here, and store some clothes but stay at the penthouse belonging to my firm when I'm in London. Wherever I go there's no difficulty over a bed for the night. Business contacts are very generous, as I expect you know." He grinned. "Almost too generous at times. I get offered some bizarre things."

Like women for amusement? She wondered. "It's often easier to go along with other people's arrangements, but I wish I could book my own hotels occasionally. Max is wonderful and smooths the way while I just put on the war paint and smile and do as I'm told, but sometimes it's a bore."

"Max?"

"My agent and far more. He's a real friend and he's wonderful at his job."

"I'm sure he is." The car sped over the reflections of green lights at the junction and turned off to the suburbs through the dingy streets and the sudden bursts of green parks that make London breathe.

"You haven't lost your sense of direction. You drive as if London was your backyard."

"It's never been that." He swung south west and left the dual carriageway, entering the stockbroker belt and open country. Another small town or an extension of London broken off for a space, pretty roof tops and gardens and an easing of the traffic made the morning lighter and more leisured. "We're making good time. Do you want to stop for coffee?" She shook her head. This was no time to sip coffee and sit face to face and talk. Carol would have to be the catalyst for memories and keep it light. I don't want to relive old times, she decided. He may feel the same and only when they could dismiss them lightly with a third person around would it be possible to talk of the past.

She glanced at him. After even this short time she could

glimpse the Paul she had once known, lurking under the bespoke suit and the sharp shirt and the well-tonsured hair that now began to rebel against the regimen of brush and skilled hairdresser. It always did curl. His hands were the same, only clean, and his grip on the wheel was light and positive.

He had been positive about so many things; about his ability to make good, about his domination of subjects attempted and discarded by his friends but absorbed by him as knowledge to be pigeon-holed away for the future, and positive that he wanted Catrina, for ever, to follow on as they were going, drifting into a relationship and marriage, for her to be his girl, his wife and his lifetime companion, with never a thought that she too might crave for the bright lights.

She snuggled back, enjoying the sun breaking out for good. The washed sky over cherry blossom was too chocolate box to be real, but breathtaking. She sighed and he tightened his lips. "Bored?"

"No. It's so pleasant to be driven for a change and to see things without having to concentrate on the road. I cover a wide area and most of the time I welcome the solitude while I'm alone in the car, but after yesterday, I'm glad to be driven."

He grinned and cut in behind a van as they reached another shopping centre. "Feel free to admire the view," he said. "Woolworth's, Tesco's, a hardware shop and a greengrocer's! Oh, and a boutique, lucky local house-wives." They left the rank of shops and the road opened out once more. He was a good driver, which was no surprise. He didn't rabbit on while he drove, but that might have been because he had nothing to say to her anymore.

The next rank of shops had a window lit from the back to throw the plastic models into relief. Catrina smiled, wondering if he would recognise her image. That had brought a smile to Max's face when he got the contract signed. Nearly every chain store had a Catrina model in the window, wearing something in which she wouldn't be seen dead. They paused to let the build-up of traffic thin and she watched the models, in a twilight gloom even when the sun shone, angular in odd poses, like ballet dancers caught off balance in a high wind.

What fun to have a green wig and a pouting bronze mouth like the one in the corner . . . not a Catrina. What a sensation that would cause if she arrived in Carol's neck of the woods like that. They'd care in a place like that. It was only a few miles from London but the impact would be as much as if she arrived dressed as she was today in a really small seaside village.

They slid to a halt at the next traffic lights and she pressed the window button. The air was good, even when faintly smelling of petrol as a large estate car drew up beside them. The air was still damp but the puddles were drying. Catrina looked sideways at the neighbouring car. The sleek lines were not new and the window was down. The driver had large hands with thick gold rings on the fingers of his left hand and one on the right. The kind of rings worn by men in Mediterranean countries and taken for granted when she visited Cyprus and Italy but rather heavy seen out of context with the country of origin.

Although the hands were clean, the fingernails were

not, and they were at variance with the man, as if he had washed his hands in a hurry but had not had time to clean his nails after a dirty job such as changing a wheel or cleaning something. The estate car swept away on the amber, jerking a little as his foot went down. Catrina glanced into the back of the vehicle and saw a bright woollen car rug wrapped round a shapeless mass on the rear platform. For a second, she was aware of a soft brown shoe and a glimpse of sheer tights. The car turned right and was lost by a furniture van.

"Paul!" He was accelerating as she clutched his arm. He swore and braked and she relaxed her hold. "Sorry, but didn't you see? There's a body in that car!"

"There'll be one in this car if you do that again!" He drove on, with a strident horn making imperious music behind him, jeering at his bad driving. "Okay." He slipped into a parking space and braked. "A body." he regarded her, his hands limp on his lap. "You saw a body?" He looked at her with cold eyes and she remembered that they were like that when he was very cross. The blue went stormy like flecked water and his hair gel was losing its hold. The old Paul was there, angry and fed up with her for making him feel small. How he must have hated any man thinking he was a motoring moron in a fancy American car that he couldn't handle.

"I saw a body."

"What kind of a body? A whole body sitting up? Part of a body? A head, a hand, an arm? I'm fascinated."

"Oh, Paul, I did see it. I'm sorry I grabbed you, but it was there. It was a bundle in the back of the estate car that stopped by us at the lights. As he left, I saw a woman's foot and leg. He went from nought to whatever in seconds flat and the rug shifted." Her eyes filled with tears as she turned to him. "I really did see it."

He looked at the bright eyes and trembling mouth. Never in all the magazines had she looked so vulnerable, so innocent. He took her hands in his and his eyes were tender. "Catty," he said. "I began to think you were dead. I saw your pictures and then I saw you and it seemed that you had died and a plaster model had taken your place, painted up to look like an angel."

She dragged her hands away. "He went that way, Paul! We have to follow him. The man was wearing a dark suit and had black hair. He wore a load of gold on his hands including a ring that looked like a leather belt with a buckle."

Paul leaned back and laughed, and in the laughter was relief and affection. "Oh, Catty, little Catty, you haven't really changed a bit. You're still the zany, crazy kid I knew. Under all that sophistication you are the same!"

"You haven't heard a word I said! We must find him."

"Cool it. Do you recall a time when you tried to tell me a man was beating his wife? You saw him against the window blind hammering away at her? You made muggins here knock on the door and say the bike was giving trouble and I needed to contact a garage, as a pretext to use the phone and get into the house."

"I don't remember," she said, but looked away.

"Oh yes you do! Don't lie to me." He laughed. "Of course you remember. He was chasing a maybug round the bedroom trying to hit it with a rolled-up newspaper, and he didn't take kindly to being interrupted as his wife was screaming that she was frightened of bats and thought it was one. You don't know what this means to me. I was so scared of you when I first saw you on the catwalk and again today against the background of that awful apartment. But you are in there. Hello, Catty," he said softly and kissed her gently on the cheek.

"But *Paul*, I did see her. I saw a body!"

He started up the car. "Carol will be expecting us. I want some coffee and I have no intention of dead bodies ruining my day." Catrina stared down the side road into which the estate car had vanished and saw that ahead was a roundabout with three turnings. She sank back, furious for her sudden panic.

It was all symptomatic of the strain building up over the past hectic months and it frightened her to feel that she might be imagining things. What was worse was the fact that it gave Paul that insufferable sense of superiority that she recalled so vividly. She was back in time and the car could have been the noisy motorbike, with him yelling at her to hold on and to sit straight or she'd have them both in the ditch. But I *did* see it, she told herself firmly.

"All right. Don't believe me. I imagined it." He was smiling and she felt as if a good hard slap across his grin might help her if not his driving, but she sat quite still. "Don't believe me, and when you read about a body wearing soft brown shoes and tights of a rather nice shade of pinky brown, you'll have to confess to the police that you made me withold evidence!"

She laughed as if it were a joke and sat forward to see where they were going. "Only another couple of miles," she said, as if he didn't know. Carol lived in a remnant of country near the commuter belt, up a lane that wasn't worth the attention of planners, so it had been left with its barns and stone houses and a few cottages that had been lovingly restored. The village was fast becoming an offshoot of the neighbouring town but the tiny haven remained intact and could shut off the world of modern commerce and movement as soon as the first rutted patch of lane was negotiated.

"I ought to come here more often," Catrina said with regret. A wet fan of leaves brushed the car window and she saw a chicken playing truant in a garden, eating the bird food. "But time flies and I never seem to have any to spare for what I want to do."

"You have today." Paul held back a strand of ivy that forgot to trail over the Elizabethan chimney stack at the edge of the brick path and Catrina walked carefully to avoid the dips in the worn surface. A hand at a window waved and disappeared, and they heard Carol call the barking dogs.

"I've shut them in the kitchen," she said firmly. "You can't have them pounding all over that nice suit." She eyed the pale silk with something like dread. "They are both covered with damp from the long grass and Rufus rolled in something nasty. The foxes are about and he loves to smell like them."

She showed no surprise that they arrrived together and she kissed Paul as if she had seen him only last week and he was always welcome. It was easy to chat with Carol there and the gulf narrowed. Catrina put her case in the hall and hung her coat on a hook behind the door

Elizabeth Daish

in the porch. "I brought tickets for the fashion show at the Manor," she said.

"Do you have to be there? I thought you wanted to relax."

"Only if it would amuse you to see it. I'm not doing anything but watching, but it isn't important if you say no."

"I don't know." Carol bit her lip. "You wear everything as if it was designed just for you, but if I tried that suit on, I'd look a mess." She smoothed her plump hips and tried to make the union between jeans and shirt more permanent. "And don't tell me to wear that thing you sent me! I have yet to discover which is the front and which is the back!"

"That was just a piece of nonsense to wear in the garden in the sun; I've brought you something wearable this time. But really, Carol, I don't know why you go on about your clothes. All the back-up team will be wearing casual clothes and some will look as if your dogs had chewed them."

"That's no consolation. I often get chewed up by my dogs."

"Coffee? Anyone going to ask me if I want coffee? I'll make it if you tell me where to find everything." Paul put his briefcase on the floor and peeled off his jacket.

Catrina laughed. "Since when have you been tamed into kitchen skills?"

"Tamed?" His quizzical smile made her blush.

"You don't live alone, do you?" It came out almost as an insult but he didn't seem to notice.

"Off and on. I travel a lot. This is really another business

40

trip but this time I was determind to look up a few old friends and see who had died."

"No flowers for me. I didn't die."

"No, you managed without me. I can't think how, but here you are." He went into the kichen and she heard him telling the dogs to be quiet. Carol hurried after him and the barking stopped. Catrina heard the voices and Carol laughing. She went to the window and wondered how it would be, living in a cottage, looking out at rain-drenched early flowers, with the drying sun hot through the glass.

She kicked a rubber bone under a chintzy settee and brushed her skirt before sitting on a straight-backed chair. Even here, on a day off, she couldn't relax in case she appeared in public this afternoon. She dared not look crumpled and it was instinct that made her take the hard chair instead of the deep armchair that looked comfortable.

Carol shut the door quickly behind her and sank into the well-worn chair. She reached for a packet of cigarettes and offered them to Catrina. "No?" She shrugged and lit her own. "Very wise." She blew smoke up in a thin line. "He seems to know what goes on in a coffee filter, so he can get on with it. He's done well for himself, hasn't he?"

"I wouldn't know." Catrina moved restlessly, her hands showing tension. "It was a complete surprise to see him again. I had almost forgotten that he ever existed." Not true, but Carol always had a nose for sentiment and drama. "What does he do? Has he a family?" The early daffodils in the ceramic pot were badly arranged and she leaned over, partly to find a use for her hands and because she loved flowers.

"He lived with a girl for a year. One Christmas he wrote and told me about her. She sounded nice. Someone from the same firm, but it didn't last. Other than that, he seems to be footloose and fancy free and never in one place for long enough to put down a root. I think he can take a breath and please himself more now as he practically owns the firm and talks of buying property, instead of using hotels so much. He does own a couple of apartments but not a real home." Carol looked about her at the warm shabbiness of her own sitting room. "I don't suppose he can manage dogs, although he adored them at one time, and mine drool all over him."

"He always wanted to travel and now he does," Catrina said.

"You always wanted to be a top model, and here you are! Two happy people."

"That's right, all our wishes granted." Catrina ignored the query in Carol's eyes. "Now, while he's busy, let me show you the pressies." She brought in her case and snapped back the clasp. The simple dress was exquisite but not so startling that it would scare Carol away from wearing it. "I think it's your size, but if you don't want it, I'll take it back."

Carol looked at the label and laughed. "I'll wear it even if it's two sizes too small. It must have cost a bomb!"

"Only an arm and a leg," said Catrina. "You want to come this afternoon?"

"I'd love to if you promise to stay with me and not desert me. I hate going to places alone and I'm the world's worst at making conversation with your rather precious friends."

Catrina laughed. "I know. Poor Louis couldn't get over your fraught face when he introduced you to his boyfriend. He began to look at him with fresh eyes, wondering if a) you were jealous, and b) if he was too awful even for Louis!"

"Coffee!" called Paul. "Come and rescue me and hold the dogs or they'll eat Catrina alive."

"Give me five minutes to change and then let them in." She fled to a bedroom that Carol kept for guests and where a couple of drawers held her spare country clothes. She changed into couturier jeans, a bright sweater and trainers. The jeans were at least a year old but she had worn them only twice. She tied back her hair in a small silk scarf and wiped the make-up from her face.

"Rufus," she said with an affectionate ruffling of damp fur. "You stink." She sat happily on the rug, avoiding the tongues of the two dogs. "And why they called you Princess, I'll never know," she said, pulling the ears of the dilapidated old bitch that Carol had rescued from the dogs' home.

"She needed a boost to her ego as everyone who saw her said 'What's that?' and we had to build her up and tell everyone that she is a princess," Carol said. "Sit up and drink your coffee. I have to light the stove and get lunch ready if we are to eat at one. I suppose you *are* eating? No diet?"

There was nothing anorexic about Catrina, she thought, but a fine-drawn air of tension that must have been there before Paul came back on the scene. It couldn't be due to his return, and even if that did affect her, Catrina was too well disciplined to show it. This tension went deeper and the beautiful eyes held an an echo of regret, somewhere behind the child-blue whites. The well-manicured hands stroking the dogs and the way she touched flowers made Carol wonder if the elegant girl missed being a mother, or at least missed not having a real home of her own with dogs or cats; but it was unreasonable to burden herself with any living thing if she had to go off at a moment's notice to who knows where.

"Lovely. Much too strong and usually I resist cream but today I shall eat everything I want and take a deep breath at the next show."

"Do you resist every temptation that might get in the way of your work?" Paul asked.

They were alone and even the dogs were quiet. Catrina walked to the back of the room and stared out of the narrow window overlooking the stream and the hill. "I'm sure that you are as disciplined," she said. "Success is satisfying but it does demand sacrifices, even if it's only chocolate eclairs." She turned and was smiling as if facing an audience, and who was to say that the smile wasn't true? "And you? What have you given up for the position you now hold? I hear that you are very successful and own a big stake in the business."

"Strange that our careers should run in parallel courses."

"Parallel but not the same," she said, too quickly.

He smiled, stiffly. "You never were much good at maths. Don't you remember that parallel lines eventually converge?"

"It depends on where you are standing. I never look into infinity." The scars were aching now as they had done when she found herself alone in a bed-sit with one beauty box, a sheaf of second-class pictures and no idea where to start. She had just read the shipping news and had his card saying that he was leaving Southampton on a one-way ticket.

She walked back to the armchair and sank into it. She was a big girl now, who could live where she liked, so long as it was in London, go anywhere, so long as it kept her in close touch with her agent and her committments, and marry who she wanted, if she could love any of the selected men who pursued her and wanted her to be a decoration in their houses, to give a bloom to their lives and a daily fix to ther egos.

"Beef casserole okay?"

"Fine," they said together. Paul laughed. "What about the hounds? Can we walk them for you and get out of your hair while you cook?"

Carol looked pleased. "That would be nice if you're sure you don't mind. I can do the veg and make a pie. Just take them up the hill and let them off there, but please try to keep them out of the stream." Catrina made a feeble attempt to offer help in the kitchen. "With those nails?" Carol eyed the pale, soft hands with amusement. "Half an hour will do but stay up there if you like it until lunch time. Here, take these gloves. The dogs pull on the leads and it's hard on the hands, much harder than peeling potatoes, so wear them."

The sharpness of the air was almost a physical assault as they took deep breaths on the way up the hill. The path was still winter muddy and rivulets of water drained down although no rain had fallen since yesterday. Catrina danced from side to side over the tiny stream, unsure if her trainers were waterproof. Paul watched her, seeing the girl he had lost and wondering at her two personalities, knowing that the years had robbed him, and that other men with far more to offer her must be there in the background. The Press gave a picture of Catrina almost married to an earl, as she had stayed in his beautiful house and looked exactly right for the part she would have to take. Would it be just another part or had that life become so familiar that it was now the real Catrina?

"Rufus, you devil! Come here." Catrina ran, ignoring the wet grass and the water soaking through to her socks. She ran up the slope to catch the dog intent on a muddy bath, and Paul ran to help her. Gasping and making fruitless grabs at the dog, they were half way up the slope, but at least they were driving him away from the water. Paul made a last effort but the dog moved off at a tangent and vanished towards the cottage, with Princess as usual a few lengths behind. "They'll be all right. Carol does let them out on their own. That's how they get so muddy."

Catrina sat on a stone, an outcrop of the rocky hill and gazed across the village towards the motorway. Flashes of light as sun struck windshields and the coloured blur of highly polished coachwork rushed by under the slender concrete bridge towards the bypass.

"Catty," he said gently.

She continued to stare at the kaleidoscope, then stood up abruptly. "Carol will be ready for us." Her smile was as bright as any he'd seen on a cover. "Even here, we can't forget our obligations," she said, and ran down the hill. "My feet are soaking and I *did* see a body in that car." She stuck out her tongue and beat him to the cottage.

46

Three

"There's no rush," said Catrina.

"All the fashion shows I've been to fill up very quickly and I end up watching the tops of heads." Carol looked excited. "Now you've got me all dressed up and done my face, I intend seeing what is to be seen."

"Sorry, Carol, but I have to arrive late, if only to give the opening a chance. Let the lights dim and we can take our seats quietly. I promise you we'll be fine. Sym will have our seats safely reserved and guarded with the lives of several members of her staff, so stop fussing, finish your coffee and don't spill any on your nice party frock."

Carol smoothed her hips. "It's very flattering. I can't think what happened to my spare tyre." Paul watched them and said nothing. All through the meal Catrina had softened and relaxed, the smile becoming less permanent and the eyes filled with real laughter, as if she claimed the day as hers, free of tensions, with the freedom to say exactly what she pleased without having to watch her image. "Is she right, Paul? Do you think they will keep our seats?"

"If they don't, heads will roll," he said sternly. "Catrina will have public hysterics and I shall cancel the order I gave to Symfony."

Catrina's smile dimmed. "So you did give her an order? No wonder she wanted me to meet you and made such a fuss about it."

"You didn't want to see me?"

"I had no idea that you were in London," she said. "I can never see anything through the lights at shows and you didn't exactly reassure me when you tried to pick me up on the Embankment! How did I know who you were? I get a lot of hassle from men who have seen my picture and say they know me." She went into the bedroom that Carol had urged her to use soon if she could take time off. The jeans were on the radiator and had dried, so she put them in the drawer with the rest of the casual clothes and wished for time alone with Carol for more than a day. If only Paul could stay too, they could walk and slop around doing nothing, but she found it impossible to suggest it.

He was walking about, talking into the handset and Carol whispered, "He has to go over some designs with Louis before he goes back to the States."

Catrina moved away from the sound of his voice talking into the phone. "He's staying? How long?"

Carol shrugged. "We'll hear more later. He didn't say, but I take it his plans include you?"

"Not really. We are in the same trade now. Coincidence and it's very good to see him again, but don't mistake forget-me-nots for orange blossom, Carol. We've grown up."

"He was asking about your pet earl."

"Was he?" Catrina shrugged and her professional smile switched on as Paul came from the phone. "Ready to go to talk to your colleagues, or do you want to wait for us? If you go now, I shall follow in Carol's car as I don't want to be there until the music starts."

"I think I'll go. I promised Hugo to look at some papers before the show begins. See you in there."

"That's the Paul I remember," Catrina said, with a laugh. "Do you remember, Carol? He was too mean to pay to take a girl to a disco. We always met inside." She wanted to giggle and to dismiss the memories as just that, childish memories. Everything was flooding back too fast and she didn't know what was possible any more. He couldn't come back now, casually destroying the ivory tower and taking over her life.

"Tell you what I'll do to prove I'm no cheapskate. I'll meet you back here and take you out to dinner before we go back to London."

"I have to be back early. Max will be wondering where I am. He isn't coming here today as it doesn't concern me in a professional way, but he'll be anxious as we have a big show tomorrow."

"I rang him," Paul said abruptly. "He knows the score. I'm taking you out to dinner."

"I think I'd better ring him now," Catrina said evenly. "I like to know what is expected of me professionally. Max deals directly with me."

"You mean he decides exactly what you should do? Christ, Catrina, don't you have any choice ever?"

"Of course. I have the choice to ring him now and to hear what I have on my schedule so that I can plan tomorrow as I like it, or voice my objections and have the schedule revised." She brushed past him to go into the hall and dialled the number. She waited and Paul went past her without another word, shutting the front door after him with far more force than was strictly necessary.

"Thought you were all tied up at the manor," Max said. He told her the plans for the Sunday show as if repeating what he was convinced she knew. "Why am I telling you this? The guy who phoned said he'd tell you."

"I don't like instructions second hand, Max. I can be back in town tonight if you like."

"He said you had a date with him for dinner. Fine by me, darling. Time you hit a night spot again and had some private fun, even if he isn't newsworthy. However, a wealthy American businessman can't be bad as a long term investment."

"Newsworthy? No press today, Max, you promised."

"Well, you know how it is. Katy was here when he phoned and she latched on to it. He asked if I had a list of restaurants in Surrey and I suggested the Ragged Bear, so he's booking a table and she may or may not turn up, just by accident."

"You pig," she said, without heat. In one way it might be better to revert completely to type this evening. She smiled maliciously as she put down the phone. If he thinks he's having me all to himself in cosy candlelight he'll be shocked to find the local Press and a stringer for the dailies watching every mouthful he takes. "Clever Dick," she said and called to Carol that it was time to go.

The car park was fairly full and it was obvious that the show was very well attended. Word might have got round that the famous model was in the district and would be there in the audience with friends. If Sym had anything to do with it, the message would have come over, loud and clear on the local wires, the church bells and by pigeon post.

It was quiet in the hall, rather like going into church, and the startled look of the vicar's daughter who was on programme duty at the door added to the illusion. She recovered and beamed, thrilled to be the one to show the famous woman to her seat but Catrina stopped her gently, long enough to ask if the lights in the main auditorium were down.

"The ventriloquist is on," the girl whispered. "You'll miss him if you don't hurry."

"We want to miss him and sneak in when nobody can see us."

"But everyone knows that you are coming here, Miss . . . Miss . . ."

"Just Catrina," said Catty with a brilliant smile. "I do mean we want to slip in? Really, really slip in and be quiet . . . ?"

"Serena," the girl said.

"So, Serena, you will help me? I'm not here on business but as a private individual and I need space."

The girl nodded and Catrina knew that she would willingly knock a hole in the wall if Catrina wanted to enter that way. Applause came to them and a buzz of amused voices. The doll gimmick was going well. Music and the lights dimmed in the huge high-walled hall that was now filled with the catwalk and small chairs, mobile lights and everything that transformed it from the sixteenth century to something quite foreign to its age and dignity.

Almost stealthily, Catrina and Carol made their way

to their seats and the buzz of sound continued unbroken. The girls on the ramp would have their moment of glory without being overshadowed by Catrina, and they were doing well.

The two white-faced dolls sat propped up by the potted plants, one on either side of the dais, and the other two dolls slowly rose from the floor beside them to gasps of disbelief from an audience that had been brainwashed into thinking they were dolls, too. One girl was confident but the other hesitated as if she had been thrust into the costume, plastered with make-up and told to follow the actions of the first living doll.

From the way she held her hands, Catrina knew that the first girl was Marcia, but the second one lacked the bold, flowing style of Patricia. She was thinner and shorter and obviously unsure of her performance. Carol was enjoying herself, sitting in the front row among the important guests where the view was the best and knowing that she was dressed in something that gave her style.

Catrina glanced through the shadows and saw that Paul was there with the two Americans. He nodded slightly and half smiled, looking as he had done when they fought and he was half apologetic. Today there had been no fight, unless he was conscious that he had presumed too much, refusing to believe that the Catrina of now was not quite the Catty he could bully into doing as he wished. She looked away, aware of the tension between them after all this time.

The clothes were good and it was amusing to watch from the other side of the walk. Sym certainly knew her clothes and the girls scented the mood of the audience as sharply as any West End impresario. Although there was high fashion, Sym knew that in such surroundings, the County ladies might be there, ready to buy less extreme numbers that would fit in with country lifestyles and the less fashion-conscious hunting and shooting community, so she had included a series of simple skirts and shirts and jackets.

From the murmurs of approval it was certain that she had done well and the less fashion-conscious would still enjoy the haute couture but dismiss it as extravaganza.

In the interval, the Americans came over, by which time the audience had almost forgotten that another attraction would be the top model Catrina, and apart from a few stares in her immediate vicinity, she was left alone. Twice, close to her, flashbulbs lit the scene, showing startled eyebrows and cups of tea halfway to lips. Catrina never ate or drank at these functions, knowing the bent humour of photographers who enjoyed catching their victims at bad moments. No spaghetti tonight, she thought.

The interval was over, the Americans reluctantly resumed their seats but Paul stayed away, talking to Louis and one of the administration staff and only sat down again when the lights were down. The last raffle ticket had been sold, the rustle of paper behind the scenes was hushed and the dolls on the dais slumped as their stuffing sagged. Once more the girls sweated under the blank white make-up and at last, the show was over.

Sym came towards her with a purposeful air. "Glad you could make it, duckie," she said.

"What do you want?" Catrina asked warily.

"Don't look like that! It's only the prizes. I told the

organiser that you would do the raffle tickets. For charity, you know." Sym looked smug.

"What did Max say? I bet he doesn't know. Did I notice a slight accent on the charity?"

"Come on, it won't take a minute."

"Go on, Catty. It is for a good cause." Carol looked elated. The son of a visiting army general was looking at her with intent and he wasn't half bad.

"It's always a good cause." Catrina took a deep breath. "Okay. But I don't have supper with the vicar!"

"You certainly do not. Have you forgotten? You have a date with me." Paul was there, half confident.

"I suppose I have to eat somewhere. Where do I go now?" Quickly, she made her way to the back of the stage and on to the jutting platform. She sighed. Louis was doing his nut with the introduction. ". . . special effort in a busy schedule, giving her services free for this very good cause." That's settled Max. Even he can't ask for a fee now and I ought to give a little. She did her stint as if it was very important and spoke to each of the winners, knowing that more tickets had been sold at the last minute to give more people a chance of meeting her. Louis had been so pleased with the show that he gave six suede belts to add to the prizes.

"Good girl," Sym said when Catrina came back between the curtains.

"What happened to Patricia? Still away? Have you checked the hotel to make sure she isn't really ill? With a do-not-disturb notice on a door handle, a girl could lie there for days without being seen."

Sym pursed her lips. "We made them check but she

wasn't there. A different tale to the one she sent us, the little cow. She told Louis that she was ill and couldn't make the show but the hotel haven't seen her since yesterday. She didn't sleep there last night." Sym looked furious. "There should be a law about men like Max. I know where that little slut spent the night! It's all very well for him. He takes it for granted that all the girls are a lot of tramps but half of them were virgins before he came on their scene."

"You really think she was with Max? I'm sure you're wrong, Sym. He knows what the shows are about and he's a pro, too. If sex came between him and business, I know which would win. Besides he wouldn't louse up your show. He's involved. Hasn't he a share in the firm?"

"So he has. Now that makes me think. Max does know Pat pretty well. This wouldn't be a one night stand in a hurry in case she got away! He was with her the night we were on the boat."

"I know he had a date but I didn't know it was her. He left me quite late."

"He seems quite turned on by Pat, as far as Max ever shows it, but as you say, he's involved with us and I've never known him act in this way."

"You didn't have a message from Max saying that she couldn't make the show?"

"The only message we had was brought by a boy from the hotel. It's a small place, family run. You know the kind of dump."

"I do know." Idly, Catrina ran her fingers over the lid of a long black box that sat on the edge of the back of the stage. "What's this? Somewhere for Louis to keep his toys?" She lifted the lid. "Oh!"

"Serves you right for being nosy," said Symfony. "That belongs to Giorgio, the vent act."

"But it's dressed exactly like the dolls in the show."

"We said we wanted the doll dressed like this and he agreed if he could keep the clothes after the show. Louis made a bit of a fuss as the dresses are expensive, but Giorgio said that if the dress was to stay in place during his act, it would have to be stapled on in places and would tear the cloth if they were removed and he had to hand back the clothes. Crafty really, but he was determined to have them. You should have seen the grotty things it wore when he brought her for audition. I don't think he'd get many bookings with props like that. He does mostly hotel cabarets."

"He should know where Pat might be. He is staying at the same hotel and she did suggest him for this show."

"I asked him but he shrugged and said he knew her only slightly. He was grateful to her for suggesting him for the show but he didn't expect to see her here." Symfony frowned. "Maybe Pat gave him the elbow if he got too close, or used him to convince the girls that she wasn't serious about Max. You know how dirt spreads like butter, and Max takes them, loves them and goes on to the next. It leaves them trying to explain why he doesn't want them anymore, unless they laugh it off and say they have another boyfriend. The rest join the cast-offs."

"I wonder sometimes why I have him for an agent," said Catrina.

"Only because he's the best," Symfony said, dryly.

"And with him, you are safe. Max would never foul his own nest or his own bank balance."

"I suppose not. Should I feel flattered?" She saw Paul saying goodbye to the Americans, who were looking without much optimism in her direction. She raised a hand and they stopped in their tracks. She bent over the edge of the stage. "Going so soon?"

"We understood that you had another pressing engagement, but very nice to meet you, Miss Catrina."

"Just Catrina," she said with the glance that had put her in the running for a title and a castle. They shifted and grinned and Paul was the boy on the bike, furious with her for riding pillion with one of his friends. "We'll be at the Ragged Bear later. Have a drink with us if you don't have to get back to the smoke." She looked at Paul and laughed. "If you change your mind about buying me dinner, I shall have company." His answering laugh had just the right amount of annoyance. A small unimportant victory, or watch it, buster, I'm not being taken for granted again? And he saw it.

She went back to the cottage with Carol, who seemed in a great hurry to feed the dogs and let them out for an evening run. "Nice date," teased Catrina.

"Could be. The bugger passed me last week when I was on my moped and didn't bother to look, but now he really seems interested. Can I have a dab of that scent you brought with you? I want to knock him cold."

Catrina gave her one of the tiny handouts of perfume and some more suitable lipstick. "You look very good. Got clean knickers and a hanky?"

"In case I get run over?" They laughed at the corny family joke.

"If I go out to dinner, I might have to borrow back that shawl I sent you. That is, if you haven't sent it for jumble!"

"A waste on me. Far too luscious. It's in the top right drawer in my room."

"Thanks, Carol."

"You're welcome." She was excited and knew that Catrina was the fuse that made her sparkle and slip out of her normal reserve. "Come and stay for a few days," she begged. "You're good for me, Catty. When is the last time you had a holiday?"

"Venice, three months ago."

Carol snorted disbelief. "Icy cold and being photographed in the mist? Call that a holiday?"

"The Cipriani was good." But she remembered the grey water of out-of-season Venice, the eerie calls of the gondoliers in the fog-bound canals and the age of the place. "I could do with a break," she admitted. "We're well up in our schedules and the pictures for the year are in the can. I've done three commercials and two interviews that don't come out until the autumn. Isn't it odd? If I died tonight, Catrina would go on as if nothing had happened for at least two years." She thought of the doll, lying in the box. It had a kind of immortality. I could die but that thing could go on living for as long as it took her operator to live and die.

"You give me the creeps! You *do* need a break. Fix it with Max or I'll ring him and say you are going out of your tiny mind."

"Perhaps I am." Carol was glowing and it made Catrina slightly depressed. "I envy you this cottage and the dogs and the village, even the curtain-twitching and the boredom. You really enjoyed today and the crummy show, didn't you? And tonight, he'll be on a white horse and you think he's romantic. Lucky Carol."

"You'd hate it here, Catty." The glow died. "Come back soon. You make things happen for me. I need you to push me out into the world. No white horse, but I do see a glimmer and I want it."

"Be careful. The way he was looking at you, you might just get it! What did you say? Top drawer?" She changed into the unruffled dress of cream chiffon, light as a dream and uncrushable, the sheer tights and the high-heeled sandals. For her image or for Paul? she wondered.

She fixed an earring as she came back into the sitting room. "I invited the Americans for drinks at the Ragged Bear," she said.

"I thought that Paul wanted you all to himself. Does he know?"

"He's spitting blood! I wasn't asked out, I was *told*, so we have company for drinks first."

"You haven't changed, have you? Just more of it." Carol left her to figure that out. "Take a key in case you're too late to get back to town and remember, you come down here at any time. In fact, keep the key and come even when I'm not here. I have to go to Margy to check she's all right after her operation, so I shall be away for a few days, starting the day after tomorrow, but feel free to come if you can manage it. The shop will send up anything you need and the pub serves very good food."

"Thanks, Carol. There's nothing I'd like better. I'll take care of the key." It sat on her palm, an unimpressive piece of metal, but it was her key to belonging as she had never belonged to the luxurious apartment in London. It made her a part of Carol's life.

"Ready?"

Catrina looked beyond Paul and laughed. "Two cars? You brought a whole crowd of your friends with you?"

"What friends?" he said, but smiled at her radiance. "You look clean."

"I bet you tell that to all the girls." So this was to be the mood. She breathed deeply. Fine. "Are they all coming to dinner?"

"No, they are coming on sufferance. They have exactly half an hour to drool over you and to drink at my expense and then off."

"Do they know? I might like them so much that I shall have to ask them to stay on."

"I've told them that we have business to discuss and you have to get back to London tonight."

"We have business to discuss?"

"We have." He called goodbye to Carol and Catrina noticed that it wasn't a goodbye, see you next year, farewell, it was as if he was coming back very soon and then again, as if coming home.

The two cars parked easily and the fragile clouds were too impoverished to cover the moon entirely and it peeped out from behind the rags from time to time, showing up the damp patches of the car park. One of the Americans was only too eager to pilot Catrina across to the restaurant but she found that his concentration slipped as he took her arm, and she did all the ferrying.

It happened all the time and it no longer made any impact. Men were bowled over and she accepted it as if someone said her photograph was pretty. It had nothing to do with her feelings and her body gave no response to his touch. Music came from the main dining room and sounded similar to the music played during the afternoon parade. Catrina kept on her thick silk shawl as she had memories of draughty corners in country clubs and restaurants and she wondered if the heating would be adequate.

The bar curved towards the dining area, with islands of velvet stools and small tables, just out of sight of the cabaret stage, easing drinkers along to eat if they wanted to see the show. Catrina sat away from Paul, her dress a white rose on the sage green velvet. She sipped mineral water and nibbled a nut. The Americans did all the talking and she sat and smiled. They'll go away convinced that I am very intelligent, she thought. They can go with all their preconceived ideas intact. She did let them know that their firms made very popular clothes for the mass market, quoting opinions from Symfony and Louis and probably adding a little for interest.

"Sorry, you guys," Paul said, looking at his watch. He put a folder on the table. "Catrina has something to look over before we have dinner and then we have to get back to town."

Tactfully, the men said that, no, they weren't planning to eat at the Ragged Bear, and they had come only to make her acquaintance, and it sure had been a great pleasure, yes, sir!

Catrina glanced at the folder. "Work?" She reached across for it but he slipped it back into his briefcase. "What do I have to look over?"

"Me! Come on, we ought to eat and we can talk in there." The waiter led them to a small table by a curtained alcove under an overhang that had once been a balcony and now served to cast shadow on the diners beneath it. Catrina sat with her back to the wall, confident that she could see everything in the room without being noticed. She doused the candle in the rose-coloured glass and her face was pale and indistinguishable to all casual observers.

"This is good," she said, and Paul couldn't know if her pleasure was for the privacy or for his company. "And I'm hungry."

Paul ordered sea food and wine and the music faded as the first cabaret of the evening was announced. Paul filled her glass and she added no mineral water. Her eyes grew soft as she relaxed. Was it the wine, the corny comedian or being with Paul that made her laugh so easily? His hand touched hers fleetingly and was taken away as if scorched by the contact, so he wasn't just someone from childhood, but someone with a healthy reaction to her beauty. He was not immune.

She wondered about the girl in America and if he still loved her. Perhaps they had quarrelled but might get together again. They had been lovers for a year, Sym said. Perhaps they had hurt each other as she and Gabry had done and the scars were still tender.

She thought about the title she had refused and the love-hate she still felt for Gabry, even if now she could never visualise his face until she saw it in a group picture on the polo field, or sailing at Cowes. They were both shadows, as Paul had become in time, but his shadow had taken longer to fade. She watched him now as he concentrated on the food. He was very macho and his mouth gave the promise of experience. No teenage fumblings and more than a hint of threat. She sipped her wine and knew that soon she would giggle.

"No more until the cheese," Paul said. "Do you still want to dance on the table after half a glass of dry white?"

"You have no right to speak to me like that," she said with unconvincing dignity, and smiled widely.

The comic had gone and a few couples danced. She shook her head when Paul raised an eyebrow and nodded towards the dance floor. "Not this one." The couples were too close together, the music nostalgic and she wanted him close, which was reason enough to stay on her side of the table. It would be possible to dance when the disco beat hit the room and they could gyrate without touching.

The floor cleared and the next cabaret act was announced. "Giorgio and Gloria, the famous ventriloquist and his beautiful companion." Polite applause and a roll of drums and the drapes at the back of the platform curved back.

"He gets around," Paul said. "I suppose it was convenient to have bookings so close together."

"Was he the one today? I didn't see the act." Catrina leaned forward to take a closer look as the lights over the tables dimmed and the spot was on the chair and table in the middle of the platform. She gasped. The doll was very good, very life-like, dressed as the other dolls had been at the fashion show. It had an uncanny resemblance to the girls who had walked the ramp, the hair dark and the face dead white over the black blouse tucked into the rainbow-coloured skirt. Neat, pendulous feet hung in shiny black low-heeled shoes.

"If it turns you off, don't watch," Paul said, seeing her half horrified expression. "Lose yourself in the powder room until it's over."

"No, I want to see it," she said. Something about the man made her skin crawl. He was dark and quite good-looking, but although his voice was musical and cultured, the foreign accent hadn't been completely over-come. His dark suit was well brushed and his shirt beautifully laundered. The audience was already warming to his personality as the strong hand held the doll with more sensuality than some men give to their women and the relaxed audience was beginning to identify. "It's unhealthy," Catrina said, unable to pin down the right explanation for her reaction.

"It's fun and he's very good," Paul said. "Even her voice is good. Close your eyes and you could believe that she is a real woman."

Catrina stared, fascinated. The man shifted the doll to his other knee, caressing the thigh as he changed over, in a way that made men grin and the women glance at their partners to see if they had noticed. Catrina gasped.

"Not you, too? Really, darling, you must know every calculated move in the game." Paul's eyes were hard. "You use enough seduction on the catwalk."

"Not that," she said impatiently. "That's ripe corn; but his hands. Did you notice his hands?"

He shrugged. "Hands? I imagine that women would think he had six but I saw only two."

"He's wearing rings. Rings just like the ones I saw on the man driving the estate car when I thought I saw a body. Or rather *you* thought I saw a body, and I *knew* I saw one. I know it's the same man and I know it was a human body I saw."

"Christ! Not that again. I thought you'd forgotten that."

"It *is* the same man."

"You've had too much wine."

"No, I haven't. I've had only one and a half glasses." The act was leaving the stage amid warm applause. Catrina beckoned a passing waiter and asked when the next performance would begin.

"There are three shows a night, madam, and the next will be in an hour."

"You can't seriously want to stay and watch that load of rubbish again?" Paul took her glass and filled it with mineral water. "What about getting back to town? I'm not wasting good wine on you if it makes you want to beat up the odd Greek, but if you are coming back with me, then drink up and welcome."

"Be serious, Paul. Suppose I'm right and it was a body in that car?"

"Then, if you had proof, you'd have to tell the police, but you have no proof. You've seen the doll and his act and you saw him in the car with a bundle in the back wearing a shoe. Right?" She nodded. "Well then, it's obvious. That was Gloria that you saw."

"It wasn't." She was a small stubborn girl sitting quite still. "It wasn't the same. The other had pretty tights and very nice shoes. Not glossy black but a nice light brown."

"So what? You said yourself that Louis dressed this doll for the show. The clothes you saw were the original ones she wore before Louis coughed up."

"You think so?"

"I know so." He smiled. "Catty, I love you when you are like this but please don't let it grow. I know you when you get the bit between your teeth. It's a relief to know you haven't changed much, but this is stupid."

"Paul?" He sighed. "Paul, when Sym told me about the clothes, she said he had been crafty enough to get them out of Louis for free. They look simple but they are worth quite a bit. Sym said he threw out the old rags as they were falling apart. The shoes I saw were expensive Italian ones of very fine leather, like the ones the girls wore at the German Schloss for the Casino advertisement. The sponsors didn't know what to do with shoes that had been worn so the girls kept them and the tights. Everyone was chuffed as it's not every day they get such a good perk. And the tights were a new issue from Dior. Can you imagine a man buying all that for a doll?"

"You imagined it. You've been in the business too long. You can't look at anything anymore without trying to guess its origin." He patted her hand where it lay on the table picking at a serving spoon. "Come on now, Catty. It's a dream, you've had a glass of wine which you usually never touch and you are tired."

"I have to know. I'm going to find out if he's the man

I saw in the car. He's come back now his act is over and is sitting at the table by the band, and if I go to the ladies' I can pass his table if I go round the tables at the side."

"And then? You can't exactly accuse him of something so ridiculous that they'd lock you away in the funny farm?"

"No, but if it's the same man, will you come out to the car park with me to look in the back of his car?"

"All right. I'll come on one condition, if you are sure that he is the man. If we look and see nothing, then you never refer to this again. I'm getting fed up with gold rings and dolls." He pleaded with his eyes. "Catty, I feel this evening slipping away and you with it. I have to get you to listen to me."

"If there's nothing in that car, I'll listen." She smiled gently. "I *am* glad to see you, Paul."

"You are? How glad?"

"*Very* glad. No other man I know would believe me." She smiled sweetly and left the table, skirting the dance floor and avoiding the bright lights. Paul saw her pause to look at her jewelled wristwatch just as she came to the table by the band. Giorgio was sitting half facing the band, talking to one of the waiters and Catrina was able to look at him closely without being observed. In fact, one or two other women had paused for his autograph on the way to the powder room and her slight hesitation looked no more than lack of courage to do the same.

"Well, what did Miss Sherlock Holmes see?"

"He's the same man. I recognised him, Paul. The rings are the same. Remember, I told you that one looked like a tiny belt with a gold buckle? And I recognised one with an onyx stone like a seal ring. He's cleaned his nails and his shirt cuffs are dry."

"I should hope so. I clean my nails too, before dining out!"

"In the car his nails were dirty and his cuffs wet as if he'd washed in a hurry. It didn't fit in with the rest of him. He takes care of his clothes and has a very good haircut, so why not finish washing his hands?"

"So the phone rang and he had to answer it? The post arrived or he saw that he was due for an appointment? You aren't serious?" He eyed her with mock despair. "All right. I'll come with you. Leave your bag or your wrap to show that we are coming back and we'll wander out to look at the moon, in early spring, in the dark, with rain threatening. Not what I'd imagined for the most romantic episode this evening."

Eyes noted their progress as they left but Catrina showed no sign of being recognised, even when a flash showed up the local reporter. She had been lucky enough to have most of the evening free and knew she must cut her losses. Besides, she was far too absorbed in her quest. Paul took her arm. "It's very dark. We shan't see a thing."

"I hope you have a lighter that works."

"With any luck, as I carry one but never smoke. What does one do with presents that no longer have a use? Seems darker than ever and there are dozens of cars here. Where do we start?" The glint of roofs stretched far away beneath the trees.

"Look for the shape. A large estate car. It's long and low and dark blue or green."

"So are many here. You forget that this is the area

where men have big dogs and lots of children and horsy wives."

"Let's walk down the main path. You look that side and I'll take this one."

"Warm enough?"

"Just. I'm glad I brought the shawl and left my bag on the table. I don't think anyone will take it. There's nothing much in it as I never take cheque cards with me at night. I lose a lot of evening bags as I forget where I leave them."

A departing car swung headlights to show the parked cars and there was no estate car where they were looking. "Good, that narrows it down to those nearer the building. He must be parked fairly close as he had to carry his gear. They may have reserved a space for the artistes here tonight."

The next car to leave showed up a long low shape that fitted. Together, they picked a way betwen the others and stood in the dark by the one they'd seen. "Now what?" said Paul. "We can't break in."

"We can look through the rear window. Where is your lighter? That should be enough."

In the small flame they could see the interior of the car. On the floor at the back there was a bundle covered with a bright blanket, and alongside was the black box that Catrina had opened on stage and seen the doll. "There," she said. "What did I tell you?"

"Full marks. You found the car! What does that prove?" Paul snuffed the lighter and the darkness was complete. "Shh! Someone's coming."

Catrina bent as if to look for something and Paul did

the same, flicking on the lighter again. "Yes, I know we came this way but I'm sure you left it in the restaurant."

"May I help?" The voice was calm and friendly. "It is so very dark I have a torch. Have you dropped something?" The beam flashed over them briefly.

"We came out for some air and I thought I'd brought my bag with me and dropped it, but I think I might have left it on the table," Catrina explained with a laugh. "I lose a lot of things."

"If you'll excuse me, I have to fetch my other doll. Are you staying for my act, Miss Catrina? I saw you only when you were leaving."

"We did see it and enjoyed it very much," she said. "I'm sorry I missed it this afternoon, but I had to stay back with friends and it was over when I got to the show. What a good idea to have dolls dressed like the models."

"I'm sorry you missed the show, too," he said and opened up the rear door of the car. He switched on the torch and asked Paul to hold it for him. Giorgio flicked back the blanket and Catrina had to force herself not to put a frightened hand over her mouth as she stared at the blanket. Carefully, he pulled the doll from under the blanket and picked it up, carrying it across his shoulder. "I have to be careful," he said. "I make sure that all my dolls are covered in the car or people would think I had a body in there." His white teeth glinted in the torch light.

Catrina gave a fairly normal laugh. "How ridiculous," she said and Paul silently handed back the torch and closed the door of the car.

"Surely not," Paul said and stood back. "Don't let us delay you. We may be in to watch the show later."

Catrina

Catrina's fingernails were digging into his hand and in response to her tug he stayed by the car. The man walked slowly away.

"Paul?"

"What now? You heard what the man said! You might have known that he'd have more than one doll. That was the one you saw in the car. Full marks for observation, darling, but there's no doubt now, is there?"

"No, I suppose not. Can you put on your lighter again? As I bent down, my shawl touched something wet. I think it may be oil."

In the light of the flame, the stain was wet on the cream silk. Paul touched it with a fingertip and the finger came away red. "It's blood," he said, and found a small patch on the underside of the back fender.

71

Four

The shadows on the walls, darker where the paint was drab, reminded Catrina of all the worst nightmares she had dreamed as a child. Vague sounds of footsteps coming and going, and doors banging. Once a metal door clanged with quite a different resonance and she wondered if it was a cell door.

The pre-cast plastic chairs were hard and discouraged anyone from sitting too long, as if anyone would want to sit on them in this place, ever. Once, this police station had been the annexe to the local vagrant casualty ward, when hospitals took in people for the night if they had no place to sleep and no money to pay for lodging, and the despair in the brickwork was there now. The new modern station was efficient and lively at times, but the misery still oozed from the walls when the place was still.

Paul brought coffee in paper cups and Catrina put her hands round the warmth. It wasn't a cold night but her fingers were icy and even the softly lined coat was stuffy-cold. The hot bitter liquid did something to rouse her but it only made her aware of growing uncertainty and depression.

"Could we go, do you think? They don't want to know,

Paul. If we left now, they would forget we had ever come here."

"We've made a statement and we have to wait." Paul looked equally as if he wished he had never brought her to the station, with the thin tale of dolls and bodies. Now, it all seemed likely that the blotting pad on the desk had absorbed and forgotten far more important and urgent matters than the one they had reported.

A young policewoman in a spotless white shirt eyed the evening gown with curiosity tinged with envy, but everyone seemed intent on something round the corner or in another department, never with them.

"Sorry to keep you waiting." A man in a crumpled suit hurried into the corridor and opened another door. "We can talk in here. Do you mind if I have some coffee?" He glanced at the half empty cups and Catrina shook her head, so the policewoman brought only one mug. He tried to look interested but his eyes were tired. "Now, Miss . . . ?"

"Catrina." She felt foolish. Everyone called her Catrina and she seldom thought of her second name. "Catrina Milsom," she said and he wrote it down.

"So that's your real name?" He sounded mildly pleased. "Well, that will settle one argument at home. My wife was for it but her friend swore that you must be Minnie Bloggs or something." So he did know about her. Had the waiting been deliberate? Make the conceited bitch wait until I'm good and ready? He leaned back, the mug of coffee in his hand and his grey eyes probing. "The Ragged Bear, I think you said, sir?" So he'd done his homework and noted what the young constable had laboriously put on his pad. "This would be for dinner and the cabaret? And you had seen the man before this evening?"

Paul brightened. The crisp approach from the unlikely-looking man was welcome after waiting for an hour in a draughty corridor. "We, that is, Miss . . . Milsom, saw him at a set of traffic lights yesterday. That's when she told me that there was a body in the back of the estate car."

Catrina looked at him, wide-eyed. He would soon be saying, "As we proceeded down past the traffic lights, Miss Milsom alleged . . ." And *Miss Milsom*? From Paul? He was acting as if he just happened to give her a lift that day.

"And the next time you saw him, Miss Milsom?" The grey eyes waited for the obvious.

"I saw him, or rather the doll he was using, at the fashion show at the manor, but that doll wasn't the doll I saw later in the car park, and it wasn't the body," she said, firmly.

"How could you assume that, just from seeing a lump under a rug? And you did see him remove a doll from under the rug last night, or rather this morning." He yawned.

"The shoes were different. The shoes on the body in the car were expensive and the tights were good fashion. The shoes on the doll he used for the act and the ones on the doll he took from the car were shiny black chain store flatties."

"I wouldn't know the difference. Is there much difference, in fact, or are you women just conned into buying the expensive names?"

"I do know my job, Inspector," she said coldly. How dare this stupid man question her fashion knowledge?

"Each to his own. I know mine, miss." He grinned. "And it's Sergeant. Sergeant Richmond." The sudden relaxation was disarming. "You seem to be very observant but how much of this was fact and how much imagination?" She blushed, sensing that Paul shared these thoughts and would never let her forget some of the conclusions she had reached on very little evidence, way back in school days.

"But there was blood on the car and there must either be yet another doll or a body, as the doll he took out had cheap black shoes and not expensive light brown ones."

The grey eyes registered approval and it wasn't all for her powers of observation. "You arrived at the Ragged Bear at what time?"

"Just before the first cabaret." She stopped. "No, that was when we went into the restaurant. We were having drinks in the bar with some American friends first."

"A celebration?"

"No, just business colleagues of Paul's who wanted to meet me. They stayed for half an hour, forty minutes at the outside, then we went into the dining area."

"Forty minutes for drinks and then the meal. Was it any good?"

"I was surprised how good it was."

"You don't expect good food and wine out of London?"

"I haven't been to the Ragged Bear for ages and it's all different now it's changed management."

"The wine was acceptable?"

Catrina began to feel irritated. What did he want

her to say? "I didn't think to bring the menu and the wine list."

The grey eyes were hard now. "You did have wine? Was it a good evening with plenty of laughter and a relaxed atmosphere, with perhaps a slackening of that needle-sharp observation and a certain clouding of memory?"

"NO! I drank mineral water in the bar and one and a half glasses of wine at dinner."

"And you, sir?"

"If you mean were we drunk, the answer is definitely not. You have only to check with the hotel people. I signed for the dinner and drinks and they know what we had."

"And before the meal? You were both at a fashion show during the afternoon and early evening, and perhaps met more friends there?" He glanced at a note. "A Miss Carol Jardine who has a cottage in the village?"

"How did you know that?"

"As I said, each to his own expertise. We do use our eyes, miss. One of our WPCs was at the show, off duty. She's a local girl and very interested in the niece of a local resident. It is niece? You seem more like contemporaries."

"That's right." She smiled wanly. It was too much to expect that her presence wouldn't be talked about by anyone who knew her family and loved to show superiority by boasting that she knew Carol. "You seem to know all about me. I've made a statement and I'm telling the truth. I'm very tired and I have an important show tomorrow so I'd like to go home."

He stood, abruptly. "Thank you for coming," the sergeant said, as if he had given her the red carpet treatment instead of the practiced neglect. He shuffled papers on his desk and a dull flush made her believe that he had finer feelings. "My wife is a fan of yours. She spends a fortune on using make-up advertised by your pictures."

"You poor man!" This was better. She mocked him with her eyes, loving his discomfort. "Better not let her watch the next commercials or you'll be taking out a second mortgage to buy perfume; and of course, I'm launching the Orchid Look."

"Christ!" he said with feeling. Paul gave a short laugh, seeing the man emerge from the detective sergeant. It happened all the time. She was magic. He glanced at the round clock on the wall with a tilt to his head that said he was running out of patience.

Catrina saw him and her lips tightened. Miss Milsom, indeed! "Sergeant," she said sweetly, the tension leaving her mouth and the smile once more perfect. "It just occurred to me that you might like to give this to your wife to show there's no ill-feeling for being kept waiting for an hour when I was volunteering information while *not* being under suspicion, and because I want you to know that I am a perfectly sane and reasonable human being." She handed him one of the tiny phials of perfume, with two tickets for the big show.

"It's a little off your beat but I expect she'll persuade you to take her, or she can ask a friend. You could attend in the course of duty, to see for yourself just what kind of a crackpot you have to deal with."

The exit was everything she could desire. The young WPC on duty was hovering, dewy-eyed, as they left, the entire staff on duty were lined up at the desk as if paperwork was their favourite pastime at four in the morning, and Paul looked daggers at Catrina's departing back.

"Home!" she ordered. "I need some sleep."

"Why not back to Carol?"

"There isn't time. She might even be out on the tiles or entertaining friends." She wondered sleepily if the date with the local money-bags had gone well, curled up in the back seat of Paul's car and went to sleep.

"You do realise that he didn't believe a word we said," she heard through the mist. "He told me that the blood could have come from anything, like a cut or a piece of meat carried in the back of the car, badly wrapped."

"Get lost," she whispered as she pushed away the night. She tried to pull the shawl over her face but of course it wasn't there. The sergeant had kept it for examination and she had signed for it, so there was no hope of getting it back for Carol. I'll have to replace it; she can't wear anything that's had blood on it, she decided.

The back of Paul's neck was good to see when she woke and he stopped the car by her apartment block. He turned and smiled. "Had a nice nap?" She nodded and yawned. "I'll unlock for you and leave you to finish your sleep. Anything I can do, like ring Symfony and tell her that you have been released from the police station after questioning? Ring Max?"

"No, thank you. I shall have an alarm call and I'll ring them when I surface." He looked tired, and almost as dispirited as the boy she had once known, when she made it clear that she wanted to make something out of her beauty and take the world by storm. She touched his cheek. "Poor old Paul, you didn't have me to yourself tonight after all. But that's the way it goes. I expect that you have the same effect on the girls who try to pin you down to firm arrangements."

"That's different."

"Not really. I like to keep promises, but I do have to do as you do, make business come first and cancel a lot of dates I really want to keep."

He put his arms round her. "We could work together, Catty. It isn't so impossible." His voice was husky and she knew the danger signs. She was weak and vulnerable and the effort to make him go was one that he would never know.

She pushed him away, gently. "Now, I need more sleep and I go to bed alone, Paul. Shall I see you again before you leave for the States?"

"Who knows?" His arms fell to his sides, he planted a kiss on her cheek that could cool an ice cube and handed her the keys. "Sleep well and be beautiful tomorrow. Too beautiful for us mere mortals."

Catrina removed what was left of her make-up and sank into bed with a cucumber eyeshade in place. It might be possible to work with a man who had similar interests. Paul had a firm hold on the American rag trade and they shared many contacts and a lot of professional knowledge. If I wasn't so involved with my own type of work we might get together. Maybe we could get together; if everything matched, in interest, love and wanting. If . . . if . . . if. It would have been so easy to slip into his arms and back into his life and pull down the curtains, saying damn to everybody who ruled her existence as they did now. But it would be *his* life, and he wouldn't concede to hers. Was love and the security of a man in the background enough?

She slept and woke to a shattering alarm, set for later than usual, but she was miraculously refreshed, her eyes clear and her skin dewy. She showered and sat by the phone with fresh orange juice and toast. Symfony was hurried and only wanted to know that she would be in time for the show.

"Thank God for some I can depend on," she said. "Louis is having a black mood again. He was furious with the girl who was second doll, but as I said, if he can't get loyalty from girls who promise and then disappear, what can he expect from rank amateurs doing their best at no notice?"

"Having trouble?"

"Patricia hasn't shown up yet and they seem to know nothing about her at her digs. She should be wearing that new line and none of the other girls have her panache for the brighter clothes. It may mean asking you to do more. Would you mind, duckie?"

"I'm booked for the special collection but if you don't tell Max, I'll wear a couple of the others, as most of this is for charity again."

"Charity? Who mentioned charity in the same breath as Max? He would give his own mother a pound in money if she gave him two pounds in solid silver. We make nothing after paying your fees."

"That I believe. My heart bleeds for you," Catrina said, dryly. "The Americans like the frock. I gave them forty minutes of close up, valuable time, and told them that it was your creation."

"You're a pal. They've been on the blower already. It might cheer Louis up when he hears what they want. See you this afternoon, and I promise no liberties with your face this time. The great public prefers to see you *au naturel*."

"Great. See you this afternoon."

Max was less helpful. "Sure you've had enough rest? This one is important. They'll all be there and I have a few people lined up for new magazine work. The Aussies have at last seen your face and can't wait to get you into the outback, and it's good weather just now, so they tell me."

"I'm not going out of England again for months."

"Next month," he said firmly. "Don't be difficult, darling. The continuity is vital and they love you. Some of the pics will be fine for next spring here, with a few added backgrounds if the Oz batch aren't British enough for our markets, and Symfony has the first samples ready for that collection."

"They want me, not love me. Quite different. They'd ditch me tomorrow if I grew two heads." She swung the silken hair away from her face.

"Two heads as beautiful would take you anywhere." He laughed. "I may be a bit late there but I shall see you at or after the show."

"Don't tell me that you're letting your private life intrude on your business? She must be something. And what about me? If I am to go down under, I must have a break. I might as well say this now, Max. I feel tense and a bit depressed and if I don't take a rest, it will show. I'm taking a whole week off. I'll be back in London

81

again on Saturday if you like to discuss future plans, but tomorrow, Monday, I'm going down to the country to relax and recharge my batteries." She braced herself for the explosion, but none came. "Are you still there?"

"Yes, I was thinking. It might be a good idea. We're very well ahead and I have some other business to see to here. I might even take a couple of days off in Paris, myself."

"Ah! I knew you had a bird somewhere. Who is it this time, or shouldn't I ask?"

"No secret and you do know. I've been dating Patricia for quite a while now and I think she'll come with me."

"Well, keep quiet about it when Sym is around. She's spitting blood over that girl. Have you hidden her away in a love nest?"

"Of course not. I can't think why Sym is uptight about her, she'll be at the show today, won't she?"

"We all hope so, but she seems to be a bit elusive and wasn't with us yesterday."

"Damn. I should have phoned her before now but I was busy. I'll check with the hotel and find her."

Catrina was relieved by his casual conviction that Patricia could be found easily, and yet she had a sensation of anti-climax, as if she had expected something intangibly more dramatic. If Max was dating Patricia, he should know where to find her. He'd had a date with her after the fashion show on the boat, so surely he saw her that night? Knowing Max, she was certain that once in hot pursuit of a girl he followed her relentlessly, until he was tired of her, or being sure that she wanted him he could afford to neglect her a little and leave her guessing for a few days.

She rolled on sheer tights, and was reminded of the shade worn by the doll in the back of the car. It was a doll, she tried to convince herself. She had imagined the shoes and the tights; probably a memory had been dredged up from her subconscious. A rare flash, identifying a girl lounging on a couch wearing pretty Italian shoes.

She glanced at the telephone and put the handset closer while she packed her bag, so that she would be there when it rang. Maybe Paul had tried to get through while she was talking to Symfony or Max, and would try again soon. There had also been the reporter who rang twice, angling for an interview, by-passing the agent so that the meeting would be informal and for no fee.

She gathered up her things with the deliberation of one who knows that one forgotten item would surely be the one vital essential to her whole make-up or dress. The shell hair-combs and the three pairs of shoes, the well-cut underwear that she wore in preference to those supplied in almost the right size; the new shades of blusher and lipstick that were wearable for a change but not under very bright lights.

Shoes. Damn shoes. Models weren't the only ones with good shoes. Anyone could have given Giorgio cast-offs for his act. They could have come from an upmarket charity shop with clothes from a wealthy district. If Patricia lived in the same hotel she could have passed them on to him if they were not comfortable. Even expensive shoes might be tight and fit only for a doll.

"Hello?"

"Sym here. Where was it you went with Paul last night? You did have dinner with him?"

"The Ragged Bear. Why?"

"We've been trying to get that vent act again. He isn't at the hotel. They say he travels a lot and only stays there when he's in the district. He did the act there, didn't he? Louis wants him back for a show next week and he's mad that we haven't another address."

"The hotel must know where to send on mail, if any." Catrina bit her lip. There was no point in telling Sym of her suspicions or about her interview with the police. She knew it wasn't easy to believe and she preferred to keep a few friends. "See you soon, Sym. By the way, have you any news of your girl?"

"What girl? Oh, Patricia." The sudden lack of interest indicated that Sym had replaced her. So she really could disappear and there would be no one to wonder where she had gone, unless Max was truly in love this time. Catrina shivered. I really do need a rest, I'm getting neurotic. Of course she hadn't disappeared unless it was into Max's welcoming bed. "You've found another girl? So you don't need me for extras now?"

"Extras? Oh, no, we can't afford that." Sym sounded surprised, as if the thought had never entered her head. "You just do your bit, duckie, and they'll be flattened. The Americans are coming again."

"They get everywhere," Catrina said lightly and wondered if Paul was with them. She packed her bags into the car and threw in an extra coat and a pair of rubber boots, ready to be taken down to the cottage. The key was in her purse and gave her the sensation of having a home of her own to go to, with her own front door key. The keyring to the apartment didn't signify, but the cottage was real.

The afternoon seemed longer than usual, or was it that her thoughts were already far away in the country. Carol had been enthusiastic on the phone. "I'll leave some food in the fridge and I'll ask the shop to send up some stuff tomorrow. I'm taking the dogs with me as Margy loves them and they will take her mind off having the rest of her stitches out. I shall stay until Friday and perhaps bring her back with me. I want you to meet her."

"Thanks, Carol. All I want to do is to sleep and watch the box and walk in the woods."

"Not nervous of living alone?"

"I do live alone. I think the cottage is more friendly than any town apartment." She asked about the date and a satisfied giggle told her that there was more to come. "Is he taking you down to Margy?"

"No, I'll need the car while I'm there, but he is coming down to see that we are all right."

"Good for you. Nice change for you to have a man about the place."

"You could do with company. Can't Paul stay too?"

"Do you really want the net curtains to twitch? You'd never live it down after I'd gone." She laughed and pleaded time running out and said goodbye. Paul hadn't suggested meeting again. He didn't suggest anything but a 'maybe I'll see you before I leave for the States'. Would there be a girl in a wide hat at the airport, running towards him in a commercial's slow motion, a Cathy to his what's-his-name in Wuthering Heights? He'd been close about his women, which might mean he was serious about someone.

The hall was full and Sym was smiling. Catrina glanced

down from the catwalk and saw the beaming face of her pet earl behind a long cigar, showing no sign of giving up the chase. She gave him a sweet smile and was glad he had come to see her. He would be a way out of the spiral of work and public appearances. He was also very kind, very sweet and very much in love with her.

A photographer caught the smile and the intent gaze of the aristocratic face with the long phallic cigar glowing up at her. Ah, well, it was bound to happen. In the front row, right, the two Americans sat, one sketching surreptitiously with an eye towards the rear platform in case Louis caught him and the other was just staring, fascinated. There was no sign of Paul.

A few seats away from the end of the ramp where other complimentary tickets found a home for excited guests, two seats were vacant. So the sergeant couldn't make it, or wouldn't let his wife attend such a tempting display of goodies. She turned to walk back, met the girl with the opposite colour scheme, the black and white negative to her positive white and black and as they passed, she saw two people come in quietly and make their way to the vacant seats at the end. Once more down to the end and she could stare into the lights as if not seeing any face. The girl was pretty, with a bad hairstyle. Could be quite a dish if she bothered. What did a detective sergeant earn and were there children?

Back again and change into the frothy confection that Symfony devoutly hoped would be worn at Ascot and the Royal garden parties. Last year she had gambled on rain and been triumphant when her crystal colours in transparent over shoes and umbrellas had flaunted over the drenched feathered hats and had protected good shoes, but this year, unless she wanted the nickname of Madame Parapluie, she had to pray to the other gods and produce something that needed a perfect day to show them off well.

The moth-like eddies of pale mist followed Catrina like wafts of ectoplasm as she projected sentiment and sex in fairly equal quantities. And they loved it. Even if the gowns were fated for a drenching Ascot, they would be bought and treasured and that was what it was all about.

The girl taking Patricia's role was very like her in build and colouring. She was good and Symfony had almost forgotten the girl who had let her down. The dark red number could have been moulded on her body, as it was intended to be with Patricia, and her arrogant dark head was perfect. Catrina looked along the row of seats and saw that the sergeant was impressed, too. He was staring at her as if to make sure that he would know her again, anywhere.

He's like that, Catrina thought. He will remember me if he sees me in ten years' time, in Los Angeles, in the tube, or in a swimming pool. His eyes make their own dossiers. He took a card from his pocket and examined it. A card or a photograph? It was too far away to see and it was time for the next change. The sportswear would be good at the cottage; nothing too hairy or bulky, with soft fabrics and earthy colours. Would Sym let her? But no, that was impossible as there would be nobody of sufficient business standing to see her wearing them and nobody rich enough to see them and buy similar clothes.

This time, Catrina smiled at the policeman and saw his

face redden. It was a good feeling to have that icy cold man watch her and want her, even if he was with his wife. It was also good to show him that in her own way she was disciplined and professional and she sensed that he would know it. Had he told his wife about the interview, or did policemen respect confidence as priests should do?

The idea of the details being tossed around at coffee mornings made her stop smiling and she looked at him more closely the next time round. He saw her staring and smiled, slowly, and she was encouraged. He wasn't hard. Underneath, he might even have a heart.

The show ended with the bridal parade featuring Louis's gown, complete with orchid make-up and tiny headdress, and small girls with freesias and mauve garlands. The net above the lights released the pastel heart-shaped confetti at the right moment and in the right place. It dropped and settled on the stage and Catrina saw one pale pink heart finding a home on the head of the sergeant. So now he did have a heart. His wife was gathering some from the catwalk edge to take away as souvenirs.

"Champagne?"

Catrina slid out of the tight gown. "Who pushed the boat out? The Americans?"

"No, your best friend."

"Julius?"

"He wants to see you."

"And you couldn't say no to a title. You are no help at all, Sym. I've told him I can't marry him and yet you encourage him each time he shows up at a parade."

"Why not? The Press love it and so would you if you

gave your mind to what's good and accepted him. Lie back and enjoy yourself?"

"I can't think of Mother all the time, and sex should be fun." She waved aside the champagne flute. "I can't drink that now. It gives me a headache. I can never drink anything with bubbles except for mineral water."

"Well, then, marry your earl just for his spa. You know he has one in Germany? Fizzy water at the wedding might be a change."

"A spa, too?" Catrina put on a simple suit of dull rose with a high-necked shirt and a plain gold chain necklace. It could have looked like any suit worn by a girl from the typing pool, but on her it was glamorous and chic. "Am I frumpy enough for his nibs and the county?" She smiled and accepted the flute of mineral water, drinking the cold liquid as if she needed it.

Two reporters allowed in with a few chosen friends, sponsors and business contacts milled round the room, and beyond them Catrina saw the sergeant. She tried to avoid recognising him. She had to meet people and be seen with her earl for the benefit of the monthly magazines and gossip columns. Surely he hadn't come to get her autograph? The tickets were enough as a gesture of goodwill, so now, please, dear policeman, she thought, can't we call it a day and forget that the zany model had a brainstorm and a too-vivid imagination?

She saw him talking to Sym. He showed his ID and Sym's eyebrows shot up. She eyed him with approval and certainly today, with a good suit and a fresh face, he was quite good-looking. Catrina went back into her changing room and asked for more mineral water to be sent in. He might be asking for more tickets or he might be wanting to interview her, so either way she wanted to be away from the beady eyes of the Press, who might even consider him a rival to the earl. What a headline in the dailies. 'Copper or gold? Policeman or wealthy Earl?' She couldn't risk it, so the sooner she saw him alone and got back to her public, the better it would be, and the papers could print what they liked about possible wedding bells and snide asides as to just how well she knew the earl and were they really just good friends.

She sipped the mineral water and, as the sergeant tapped on the door and entered, his gaze flickered over the sparkling glass. "Why, Sergeant Richmond!" she said. "How nice to meet again." She reached for a fresh glass. "Do join me."

He hesitated and then sat down, watching as she poured. He sipped, and his surprise was comic.

"It's water!"

"Of course. I never drink anything but mineral water until dinner and then a limit of two glasses of dry wine," she said distinctly. She took away the glass, having made her point. "Have some of this. They tell me it's the best."

He sipped the champagne and grinned. "Better, but I'd as soon have beer."

She glanced at her watch. "Is this a social visit? Did you pull rank to get in here or have you decided that I'm not a hallucinating idiot?"

"A bit of each. I want you to go through again every-thing you remember about the dolls and the events you described."

"Now?" She saw Symfony twitching in the doorway. "I can't come away now. I have a horde of rabid reporters wanting to get back to their offices with the copy, and a friend to see."

"The one with the cigar?" She nodded. He didn't miss a lot. "Where's your boyfriend?"

"Don't you read the papers? The Press have it that I'm engaged to the earl."

"You don't love him." He went red. "Sorry, I thought the other one was more your style."

"Paul is an old friend of the family from way back." She sipped more water. "He's due back in the States soon, and he was here mostly on business and to see my aunt, Carol, the girl in the cottage."

He stood up. "Do your stint and we can talk later, but it has to be today. Can you suggest somewhere quiet?"

"I was going out to dinner tonight, and tomorrow I'm going to the cottage for a few days' break."

"Could you make the cottage tonight? I can join you there at ten if that gives you enough time."

"I suppose so. Is it important? Last night you were less than polite about my story."

"There's been a development. Have you mentioned this to anyone here? Or anyone at all?"

"No, I don't think so. Paul isn't here, but I doubt if he'll even want to remember last night. I seem to embarrass him now just as much as I did at school."

"And you didn't talk about it on the phone to any-one?"

"I've spoken to a lot of people on the phone today but not about that. Sym has been trying to contact the man who did the ventriloquist act and asked me the name of the Ragged Bear but I didn't mention what went on in the car-park, and Max seemed to think he might be here later this afternoon after a bit of nooky with a girl who models for Sym and has been a bit of a pain, not turning up for a show."

"He isn't here?"

"I haven't seen him. Perhaps she said yes, and they've gone off to Paris. He did say that he might go there for a couple of days, and I assume he wanted to take her with him and they've gone without telling anyone."

"Paris?"

"Why not? It's a little early for pavement cafés but quite good for a dirty weekend."

"And the girl? Who is she?" His face was taut and his eyes grim.

"Patricia, the girl who messed up Sym's arrangements." She smiled. "If you want a description, you saw the new girl, with dark hair. She's very much like her. Sym was lucky to replace Pat with such a striking likeness."

"Lucky? Luckier than Pat, I'd say."

"What do you mean?"

"We found the body of a young women, half hidden in bracken on the heath a few miles from your aunt's cottage."

"Do you know who she is . . . was?" Catrina whispered.

"Not for certain and it may have nothing to do with what you saw, but we have reason to believe that she is the girl you described." Catrina gasped. "Go and get rid of your friends and drive down to the cottage. By that time we'll have more details but I must talk to you again." He hesitated. "Until we do know more, I must insist that you say nothing of this to anyone."

"What if Max rings? Can't I tell him, as he may be worried about Patricia."

"Least of all, Max. He may have been the last person to see her alive."

Five

She watched him with interest and thought that if he bit his lip once more, he'd strike blood. "Don't eat yourself," she said. "Are you that hungry?"

Detective Sergeant Richmond grinned and relaxed. "Yes, are you?"

"Bacon and eggs?" This was an absurd dream. It could be nothing more. How Carol would raise her eyebrows if she knew that Catrina was entertaining a police sergeant to supper at ten thirty on a chilly cloudy evening in her cottage.

"Let me help," he said uncertainly, and stepped towards the kitchen door.

"Do you help at home?"

He gave a rueful grin. "Only when Wanda isn't about. She complains that I never wash the pans properly and I turn the heat up too high."

"Then keep out of my way. You can talk from the doorway while I show you that I'm not just a pretty face." She reached up to the shelf for the frying-pan and knew that he was watching the line of her breasts under the oyster silk lounger suit. It was a good feeling to have a man around the kitchen who was no threat, but was there only in the line of duty. Were policemen content to look and not touch? He has a wife to supply the rest, Catrina thought. Pretty and sexy, and he was obviously a very normal male.

"Wanda? Was that the girl with you today? The Orchid look will suit her," she said maliciously. "Did she pick up a price list?"

"She did." He tried to look grim, but his pride showed. "Her birthday soon so I might get some."

She handed him the breadknife and he cut the bread into precise pieces before putting them in the toaster. The bacon curled and shed fat over the eggs. "Sunny side up for me," he said, and looked in drawers for knives and forks.

"We'll eat in the sitting room. It's warmer and more comfortable there. Look in the fridge. There should be beer. Carol was optimistic yesterday and ordered some as she thought she might be entertaining and he looked like a beer man."

He found the cans and pulled a tag, pouring the beer carefully and with evident satisfaction into a glass tankard. "That would be Mr Michael Bane?"

The fat spluttered and she turned down the heat. "You know about him, too? Is there anything about this cottage and the people connected with it that has escaped you, Sergeant?" Somehow this was the most disturbing thing of all. Who had been asking questions, keeping tabs and probably following everyone who knew her? "I feel like a criminal on the run," she said. "Do you always go into such detail about people?"

He took the tray from her and put it on the table by

the electric fire. Logs lay in the huge wicker basket and the fire was laid in the wrought-iron grate, but Catrina showed no sign of wanting the homeliness of a log fire. The one thing he missed about a modern house was the lack of open fires. He sighed. Maybe the electric fire was best. To sit here with a beautiful woman by a relaxing log fire might be more than flesh and blood could take. He tried to think of Wanda but could see nothing but this lovely woman tucking into bacon and eggs with all the enjoyment of a hungry child. "We like to be thorough," he said and handed her the tomato ketchup.

She knew she would sleep badly now, so the temptation of hot strong coffee with cream was irresistible. They sat on opposite sides of the fire facing each other and Catrina watched him take another two lumps of sugar to add to his already sweet coffee. She wondered if he did that at home and if his wife reached screaming point when the spoon rasped through the undissolved grains of sugar. "How long have you been married?" she asked. He told her three years. "Any children?"

"One little girl of four." Naughty sergeant, she thought but resisted the challenge to laugh knowingly.

The intrusion into his private life made him sit up and realise that he was the one to ask the questions and should get on with it before this luscious creature stole his heart entirely, complete with his thought processes and his sense of duty.

"About Giorgio," he said, and brought out a notebook. "Tell me again everything you noticed about him." He referred to his notes as she spoke. "You say the body in the car had milk chocolate brown shoes and special tights? You are sure of that?"

"Wait a minute," she said and went into her bedroom. She returned with the tights she had worn earlier that day. "She had tights like this."

He fingered the soft sheer silkiness, still bearing traces of her skin perfume and the faintly erotic female scent. He dropped the tights on to the table, stirred by the contact.

"Exactly like these?"

"I'm certain. It's a new shade and very expensive. I have no shoes like the ones I saw but the sides were undercut in a comma shape following the line of the foot and leaving the rest of the shoe plain."

He opened his case and brought out a shoe. "Like this? The damp has made it darker."

She backed away, putting a hand to her mouth to stop the retching sound. "Where did you find it?"

"On the body of the young woman in the bracken."

"Just one shoe?" He nodded, and Catrina was pale. It was unfitting that a dead girl should descend into death wearing only one shoe.

"Just one," he said. "They searched a wide area and found nothing more." He turned it over. "She had been dragged over rough ground but the earth where she was found was wet and tacky. No mud on the shoe except some fresh that was thrown up by the rain the other night."

"So she wasn't killed on the heath."

"I'd say she was killed indoors somewhere or of course, inside a car or van."

"So it was Giorgio?"

"Not necessarily. We know you saw the body but we have no proof as to how it got there. Anyone could have put it there before he went to the show and he could have discovered it and dumped it, thinking he'd be framed for the killing."

"But he knew Patricia and they stayed at the same hotel. She got him the job with Sym," Catrina said in a tight voice.

"That's for certain, and she fits the description you gave me and the one from the hotel, but there was nothing more to connect them; in fact the hotel manager said that she tried to avoid him as he presumed too much when she felt sorry for him and tried to help. He wanted to get really close and she backed off. She had to be quite rude to him one day when he tried to block the stairs and keep her talking, so it seems unlikely that she would enter his room willingly or let him into her room."

"You've searched her room?"

"Of course. We went over every inch but there's nothing there to indicate a struggle, or an accident and certainly not a trace of blood."

"So he didn't do it there. What about his room? He could have tricked her into going there, or even used force to make her go there."

"I think she was a big strong girl who would never go willingly with any man she didn't trust and who she had no need to encourage for business purposes."

"So what do you think happened? You searched his room and found no blood. What about my shawl? It was blood, wasn't it? Not from someone's lamb chops?" She shuddered.

"Group O which adds up to half the population of England."

"But it was human blood?"

"Yes." She poured more coffee and he added sugar and absentmindedly stirred it again and again. "It doesn't necessarily add up. That's another thing in his favour. We can't prove much from the blood. It might even be his own."

"What do you mean?"

"Patricia was strangled, and she had a few bruises indicating a struggle, but there was no other sign of real injury and no blood loss."

"So the blood isn't a clue." She felt deflated. "But he still seems to me to be the main suspect. It was in his estate car that we saw her."

"You saw her," he corrected. "And we've done some other checking. She had a date with another man that evening. Your agent, Max Gregory. He saw her after he left you that evening and you told me he had a date at that time."

"It couldn't have been Max. He may be a lecher but he's not violent. That I refuse to believe. Besides, he told me that he was going to Paris with her. He was expecting to see her today after the show. He was expecting to see her *alive*."

"And make you think he was on the level and so hide his tracks."

"That's stupid. You can't know what you're saying. Max is my friend as well as my agent and business manager."

"He's efficient?" She nodded, wondering at the hardness of the policeman's eyes. "And very good at getting what he wants?"

"That's his job. He has to be . . ."

"Ruthless? Having little regard for the feelings of others if he can get his own way by being hard?" The words came sharply and she recalled times when she had hated Max for his drive and the way she had to give in over bookings that he said were important but which she didn't want to do.

"In a way, but only in business."

"He plays the field and drops girls when he's tired of them. What if he had a fight with Patricia because she had more courage than most and wouldn't play? She might even have played the old wedding ring before bed trick."

"He wouldn't kill her. He would snap his fingers and at least three other girls would be panting for his attention."

"For attention and the means to further their careers." She nodded, less confident now. "Why have you never slept with him?" It was an outrage but one she had to endure.

"It just never happened. I didn't want him and there was no need. I imagine that he sees me as something apart. I suspect that I'm business, not bed-fodder." She tried to smile. "We really are good friends and I'd trust him anywhere."

Gerald Richmond leaned back and eyed her with speculation. "Tell me, how did you meet? Did he help you when you started out? When you were unknown and had nothing?"

"No." Catrina frowned. "He saw some takes with me in the picture as a girl at a table having drinks at a party." It was all coming back now. Max had rung her to ask if they could meet and she asked around and found that he had some very impressive names on his books. She also learned that the most famous of his clients was leaving him to get married and would be gracing the shires instead of the catwalk, as her future VIP husband objected to her doing anything more laborious than sleeping with him, rearing children and having every luxury showered on her.

"We met and he said he could make me famous," she said, simply. "And he did."

"But were you completely unknown then?"

"Not really. I had been noticed and I had three contracts lined up, but Max took them over and made them pay me far more than I'd have dared to ask. As soon as the fashion houses and magazines knew that Max was handling me, they took more notice, and knew that he never backed a loser."

"That other client who left to get married. She wanted to come back to him after the divorce, didn't she?"

"You dig too deeply, sergeant."

"He refused to have her back, I believe, as he didn't want your career to suffer by her return. He was doing very nicely out of you, wasn't he, and you were younger than her?"

"She wasn't good at film work," Catrina said, feebly excusing him. "She also had a bad temper and was difficult, so a lot of people were glad to see her go."

"And if you began to slip? Would he be looking out for another hopeful girl with a new look?"

Catrina laughed. "Everyone in the trade knows that it can't last. It has to end sooner or later, so let's not get sentimental about it, sergeant. Max wouldn't be doing me any favours if he tried to push an image that the public didn't want to see."

"And you don't mind?"

"How can I mind about the inevitable?" Her smile was gentle and sad and he thought the photographs had never caught such beauty and poignancy. Then she laughed. "Would you give me another six months? A year?"

"I'd give you for ever," he said and his face turned bright red.

"More coffee? What now, sergeant? Is the questioning over?" She glanced at the clock and as it drew near to midnight, the telephone rang. She raised her eyebrows. "Someone ringing Carol at this hour?" She lifted the receiver. "Arbutus Cottage."

The sergeant started to his feet as he saw her expression and she put a hand over the receiver and mouthed, "Max." He put a finger to his lips as a warning to be discreet. "Max! What are you doing? It's midnight and I was on my way to bed."

"Catrina! I've had one hell of a time getting you. You told me it was tomorrow that you'd drive down to the cottage."

"I thought I'd drive down tonight and really relax. Why aren't you at Orly or stashed away in a cosy Paris hotel? Didn't she bite?"

Sergeant Richmond nodded approval, admiring her poise and lack of hesitation. Quite a woman, he decided and wondered what his wife would think if she knew he was having supper with the most beautiful woman he'd ever seen.

"I can't understand it. I tried to ring Pat's hotel again

and they wouldn't tell me anything. I began to feel I was talking to a policeman and not the usual porter. If he's the new one he'll have to watch it. He was very nosy and not very polite. I was to have met her last night but she didn't turn up and she wasn't at the hotel. I can't get hold of Sym and I heard that Pat had been replaced in the show today."

"She didn't go there, either, and Sym had to get a substitute. When did you last see her, Max?" I have to know, she thought. I can't believe that Max could do anything as bad as murder but I have to clear the air. She was conscious of the sergeant's frustration as he could hear only her side of the conversation and there was no other telephone link in the cottage that he could use to eavesdrop.

"I left you after the reception on the boat and then I met her in her room. I stayed for a couple of hours and left as she was anxious to look her best for the show, even if she might be covered with that awful white make-up. She was very taken with the doll act and mentioned that Sym had decided to employ the ventriloquist. She said he was a bit of a creep but down on his luck. Very warmhearted, is our Pat, but I don't like being stood up."

"Well, I don't have her here. Where are you now?"

"I'm at my club and I think I'll stay for the night. What's going on, Catrina? Do you know, I think I'm being followed."

"Some resentful lover or husband? Maybe a private eye wanting evidence?"

"Not again! I can't think of anyone. I've been a good boy lately."

"What about Patricia? She may have someone who could be jealous."

"No, she came down from Scotland a month ago and hasn't met many people."

"She knows you. Surely a girl as attractive as that must have a lot of men friends."

"No. We met right away and it was right." Catrina felt sad. "This time," Max went on, "I might have stuck but it seems that she doesn't want to know." His laugh had a savage undertone. "Funny. Max Gregory, the girls' best friend who never gets caught, found a girl he could live with and what happens? She gives me the elbow."

"And you accept that?" She held her breath. "You'll let her go?"

"Hell, no! I have to see her, Catrina. If Sym rings ask her to contact me and try to find out where Pat has gone. If she's gone back to Scotland I'll take my break there." He was either sincere or a very good actor. Max, the man who loved them and left them, seemed to have fallen in love at last.

"Did someone follow you to the club?"

"Yes but this was another car."

"More than one car? Isn't that a little paranoiac of you to think that, unless there is one on day duty and one for nights?" She glanced at Richmond's puzzled face. "My, you are popular." Richmond scribbled DESCRIBE and showed it to her. "Did you recognise the cars?"

"I was followed earlier by a dark green estate car and I'm almost sure it's the same one that followed me when I left your flat after the reception and went to see Pat. I thought he was travelling in the same direction as us when I took you home but he parked on the other side of the road out of sight of your windows and did a U turn to follow me after I left you. I was a bit relieved as I thought that he might be the guy who tried to pick you up, but he vanished after I parked by the hotel and went up to see Pat. He could have gone on further, parked in a side street or used the underground car park at the hotel."

"And now you say there is another car?"

"Yes." He sighed. "You may be right about the private eye but my conscience is clear, or almost. It's a modest family type car parked on the other side of the road and the driver has fed himself Chinese take-away and a can of beer. He can get stuffed. I walked to the post box to check and he nearly choked. Now, about today and that little job I suggested. I'm not going to Paris on my jack, so we can do that now. Have you got your gear there? I can pick you up at the cottage but we ought to start early."

"MAX! I am on holiday. I am staying here with . . . a friend and I have no intention of doing any work this week."

"The guy with the Americans? You wouldn't do anything daft like sloping off quietly to get married, would you? When that happens we want the full works and maximum publicity. The glossies are angling more to the bridal bit than living together now we're scared of Aids, and while a year ago marriage would have ruined your image, now it would be fine. In fact, the whole business is popular just now. They even show pregnant women and women holding babies, would you believe?"

"I have no such plans," she said. "Are you going to try to locate Pat? You sound now as if you have lost interest."

"I tried to put her out of my mind, but hell no, I want that girl. She had no right to walk out on me after we had got so close."

"Maybe she didn't walk out. She might be ill or detained in some other way." Catrina sat down, her legs suddenly weak. Such a way to be detained, with only one shoe.

"I'll try the hotel again and go there tomorrow morning to check on her. By the way, the guy with the Americans rang asking where you were, so who the hell is with you now, if it isn't him?"

"Goodbye, Max. Take care." Firmly, she slipped the instrument back on its base, cutting off the annoyed voice.

"Good girl," said the sergeant and she was pleased enough to blush.

She told him all he couldn't guess from the one-sided call, and he frowned when she mentioned the estate car, then grinned at the description of the other car and the man eating the Chinese take-away. "Max said the estate car could have gone into the underground car park belonging to the hotel. It's really for residents only."

"Christ! We didn't know there was one. The family car is ours. We thought it best to keep an eye on him. Ferny makes that car stink with Chinese and curries and the other lads have to bring deodorisers if they're on surveillance after him." He looked up, sharply. "Why did you tell him you were here with a friend?"

"I don't know. Suddenly I didn't want anyone, not even Max, to think I was here alone, and I wished that Carol had left the dogs with me. Don't get me wrong. I trust Max, but I find myself in a rather unusual situation. I suppose in a way I'm what you people call a kind of witness."

"Can you get someone to stay with you?"

"There's no need. The cottage has good locks and Carol makes sure that everything is working. She lives alone all the time."

"And you really don't mind being alone here now?"

"I'd rather be alone." She smiled and he rose, pushing his coffee cup further on to the tray. "You have my number, Sergeant, and I think you wrote the number of the station on the memo pad."

"I'll add my home number. Ring at any time. If I'm not there, Wanda will know where to contact a squad car by radio and I'll be here before you know."

"You may be miles away."

"No, I'll be around." It was like a warm comforting hand, with strength and friendliness. "Lock up carefully after me and don't talk to strange men."

"Sergeant," she said gently. "It was Patricia he was after, not me. I'm quite safe. Who would want to come here?"

"I hope that's so, but be careful. Assuming for the moment that we're thinking of Giorgio, you did see the man at the traffic lights and he could have seen your surprise in the rear-view mirror when turning the corner. He must have recognised you when you were waiting for the lights to change and you were side by side. You were near to him as Paul's car is American with a left-hand drive."

He eyed her with speculation. "You're not exactly anonymous. You take it for granted that men look at you

107

and anyone who's seen a glossy mag must recognise you in public. Giorgio knows a lot of people in show business and must have seen you many times." She shook her head but he went on. "You were at the Ragged Bear and in the car-park there, peering into the back of his car. He has only to add it up and what does he get? Not just a witness but a key witness."

"But they said at the hotel that he had left. He must be miles away by now. If he killed Patricia, he might even have left the country."

"I'll make a phone call now, if I may. It would be a relief to know he's been picked up for questioning and they may have fresh information."

"And Max?"

"He can stay until we have more to go on. I doubt if he's involved, but my man will stay in that car eating junk food until we are sure." He dialled a number and asked for Sergeant Hickson. Catrina listened to the grunts and odd words that made up Richmond's side of the conversation. At last he finished and stood looking at her. "Did you notice anything strange about Giorgio's face or voice when you saw him in the car-park?"

"What do you mean? I don't know the man so how could I say what was different about him?" She thought for a moment. "He seemed to have a cold, or rather was getting over a cold and his nose was blocked. I was surprised he did his act so well if he had catarrh."

"You really are observant."

"So he has a cold. Are you going to run after him with aspirin?"

"No, but it does seem to make Max whiter than white

if he has no cuts, scratches or a nose bleed. One less man to worry you. Forensic have found blood in the girl's hair and a spot on her shirt, but it isn't her blood. It's group O and they are working on it to find out more. They found mucus, as if it came from inside a nose, and an eyelash that could have been washed down inside the nose through the tear duct. He had a nose bleed."

"They found an eyelash?"

"They're very thorough." He grinned. "If I get anything more, I'll ring you. Sleep well." He hesitated. "And thank you."

"For what? Bacon and eggs?" She watched him go out to the car and saw the rim of light from behind a cloud where the moon fought for a last glimpse of the world before dawn overtook her.

Catrina locked the door and checked all the windows. Bed was soft and enveloping and she sank into a deep sleep almost at once, into a dream where dolls ranged along a wide windowsill, their faces staring at her in unwinking derision. We are all dolls, being manipulated, pulled about for the pleasure of others, used as ornaments, expendable, she decided, and woke with tears in her eyes.

She tossed aside the bedcovers and shivered. It was cold in the room, but there was nothing outside the cottage to frighten her. The dawn was fresh and young and peaceful except for the drone of a car engine going uphill and the drone of a motorcycle that came from miles away like a frantic wasp and died away after five minutes, way over the hill.

So there were people out later than the Sergeant or they

may have been people going to an early shift at work. I wonder if his wife gave him hell for being so late, she thought, but he had said she had been a policewoman, so she knew all about it.

She made coffee at seven and wished that the dogs were there to be walked. The milk van whined along the lane and she heard bottles clinking as milk was delivered on the back step of the cottage. She pulled on rubber boots and leg warmers and added two more layers of woollen sweaters before opening the back door to take in the milk, then decideed to leave her walk until after breakfast, but she went to the wood store and brought in more logs in case it rained later and she needed a good fire.

A large tom cat ran to her and rubbed against her legs, insinuating himself into the kitchen. "So it was you who woke me at some ungodly hour," she said. "I heard you yowling and fighting." She stroked his unremarkable striped fur and asssumed that he lived in the next house a quarter of a mile away, and he knew that the dogs were away.

He was male and arrogant and tried to steal her scrambled eggs when she went back to the kitchen for more coffee, so she put a saucer of milk down by the electric fire and settled down to the homely sound of loud purring and lapping. "I'd like a cat and two dogs and perhaps a baby," she said. She shook away the cosy thoughts, sweeping them into the rubbish bin with the crusts. Later, she could have her animals and perhaps a marriage and a family, but later.

The phone rang and she smiled as she heard the caution in his voice. "Paul! I thought you'd left for the States."

"I didn't say when I was going."

"No, you didn't, but you didn't say how long you were staying or that I would see you again."

"Max said that you were at the cottage." He couldn't seem to find the right words. "He said that you were resting, taking a break. I know that Carol is away. He said . . ."

"Max told you that I was here with a friend."

"Yeah."

"I didn't want it known that the beautiful Catrina was all alone in a lonely cottage! You know what a loudmouth my agent can be and his contacts with the Press." She laughed. "But he was right. I do have a companion. I have this distinguished-looking male with me, sharing my breakfast and purring down my neck just now. No, you've had enough milk!" She laughed. "Listen."

"A puma or a cheetah? It sounds pretty powerful."

"Smells a bit, too."

"May I come to see you? We could walk and take to the hills."

"A pub lunch, and a bar of chocolate while we walk?"

"I hardly ever eat a pub lunch while I'm walking." The light was growing and she could almost imagine his face, the face of the boy with apples in his pockets to entice her out into the mushroom fields.

"I'll be here. I was going to walk alone but I'll wait for you if you don't take all day. How long will you be?"

"Five minutes."

"Not in London?"

"Your devoted sergeant rang me. He has work to do and wanted you kept under surveillance."

"He didn't say that!"

"No, he just hinted that you could use come company."

"And you obeyed the law."

"No, I'm not that public-spirited. I'm coming because I have to talk to you."

"You have?" Her voice was almost lost.

"And to apologise. The sergeant told me about Patricia. He thought that if you talked to anyone about it, it had better be me. Safer, he said."

So he wasn't coming just to see her and to float on a cloud of shared memories. It was a telephone call that had made him get up early, and not his impatient desires. "Thank you, Sergeant Gerald Richmond," she said flatly, and shoved the cat out of doors before he sprayed the kitchen.

She put water to boil, knowing that Paul had a deep empty well that needed a constant supply of coffee to fill it. She watched the filter drain and started when she heard a car stop, lifting the edge of the window curtain and recalling what Carol said about curtain twitchers. She opened the door, wondering at her joy in seeing him. "Hello," she said. "Coffee? I've had breakfast but I can get you something to eat." We no longer kiss; not even the little kiss on each cheek that means nothing, she thought.

"Coffee would be fine," he said. The cat was yowling again. "I don't think much of your choice in bedfellows," Paul said.

"Oh, he has certain advantages. He never takes a real liberty, only where food is concerned, and I can turn him out physically when I'm fed up with him." He glanced at her and she sensed that he took this as a hint to keep his distance. "Cream?" she said.

The sharp rattle of the letterbox made her look in the hallway. She came back with the local newspaper and the national daily that Carol took. "They've released the news about Patricia. No names as yet and the usual about police making enquiries and anyone seeing a car in Recket's Wood, etcetera."

Paul took the paper. "And a very good picture of you with the large cigar-carrying earl. Does he smoke in bed, I wonder?"

"Very funny. He's really sweet. I could do a lot worse, they all tell me."

"Not all. You'd hate the life, Catty."

"I could go on my own terms, Paul. That matters a lot. I can marry him and have my own design studio. Don't look so amazed. I have a flair for design. Louis showed some of my stuff under his label and it went well. I could make a career out of that even if I gave up the catwalk and the glossies, or they gave me up."

"Let me have first refusal. We can use new talent and your name would sell them even if the seams didn't hold."

"My seams would hold. Now, let's not talk of work. I want to climb that hill and then go down to the pub in the dip by the village. I think it's still there. If they've tarted it up out of recognition, I shall spit."

She picked up an anorak that belonged to Carol and pulled it on over her other layers.

"Who would think what lies under all that lot?" Paul

grinned and caught her hand, swinging it as he had done so long ago. "Catty, have you ever thought you were on the edge of a great discovery, some great truth that will revolutionise your life and thoughts?"

"Often," she said. "Then I wake up with a spot on my face or I turn an ankle on the ramp."

"Seriously, I felt like that when I went to America, but it was a black truth then and I thought the vibes were for disaster, but I survived. I felt it again when I was made managing director of my firm, and that was good, and I felt a tingle when I landed at Heathrow this time."

"You have done well," she said. The polite remark hid the inner tumult and she wondered if it was only success that gave him his kicks now.

They reached the grassy level near the top of the hill and stopped. Below them lay the toytown view of the village, with the cars travelling slowly along the one-way system, and Catrina kept her gaze on the moving cars.

"This time it was because I knew we'd meet again, Catty."

"I've been here for ever," she said. "You took your time, and we've both had other interests, other people."

"I had to try to live life without you." He tightened his mouth and she was aware that force and a certain ruthlessness had taken away the soft brashness of youth. "I almost married. We lived together for a year but it was hopeless. All those bloody magazines smiling your face at me. I even heard you on a chat show and wondered where Catty had gone." He fondled the soft hair, lying over the deep collar and kissed her eyelids. "Catty, is it true? Have I found you again?"

She ached for his kisses, for his body, for his love, but the thick clothes made a barrier to contact and her mind held back, unable to forget the miserable years. "Why now, Paul? It's been a long time."

"That's in the past. We've had lovers but without each other it didn't work. Now we're together and could have a wonderful life. We're both successful; we could have the perfect partnership in every way. I love you, Catty. I loved you long before you had your teeth straightened, and I can't think what kept me away from you for so long."

"I wondered too."

"You do love me. I know you do."

"I've loved you in the same way, Paul, but here we are, grown up and perhaps too experienced and world-weary to go back to what once we knew and had." She kissed his cheek. "I shall always love you, Paul, whatever I do, whoever I marry and whatever life gives me, but I can't say now what I want. We may be fooling ourselves. We may not be compatible after all these years."

"Leave the door open, Catty. We can take time. There are things to be settled. Your lifestyle scares me. Could you ever leave it, Catty?"

"It's back to that. I give up for you."

"We go ahead as partners but you change a few things in your lifestyle. That's not the same. You say that you have a limited time in your career and you've given me a hint of what you want to do to follow it. Just make it sooner and live a little."

She turned in his arms and rested her head against him, longing to give in and stay with him, cossetted and loved and domesticated like a tamed white doe. She looked down at the stream flowing across the bluff and through a small channel down to the valley. Cars waited by the one set of traffic lights and took their waiting patiently. A long estate car flowed on at green and Catrina stood quite still and tense. "Paul, look down there."

He watched the line of moving cars as they gathered speed. "You have cars on the brain," he said, cross that the spell had been broken. "All right, it was similar. I saw it too, but he can't be here now, if he's the killer. Would you hang about if you thought you'd be recognised? They have no proof that he killed the poor girl, but he doesn't know that. I'd be far away by now if it was me."

"He might be trying to do something here. He may want to tie up some loose ends." She tried to sound natural but could hear the sergeant telling her to be careful. She was a witness. "I want to call the sergeant," she said. "I think he ought to know." Already she was walking quickly down towards the village, the soft spongy earth soggy beneath her boots, the sun slanting into her eyes, and Paul with a black cloud of frustration making him swear softly as he slipped and tried to catch up with her, the soles of his shoes city-smooth with no ridges.

"Wait for me!" he called. "You could telephone from the cottage later. He's gone now, if it was him."

"I can see a phone box and they don't have vandals here so it may even be in working order," she said, slowing slightly so that he wouldn't lose his dignity completely by falling on the muddy grass. "Come on, I need you," she added.

"Well, thanks! Glad to be of some use."

"I didn't bring any money, so I hope you have some loose change for the telephone," she said with a sweet smile.

Six

"Slow up, or the whole village will turn out thinking you are on fire," Paul suggested. Catrina made for the red telephone box that the village had managed to retain after many attempts by the Post Office to change it for the characterless glass and steel edifice that was becoming the norm. "You see! One of the natives is very restless," Paul said, and grinned.

The waving arms of the vicar's daughter made Catrina pause as she realised that the girl wanted to speak to her. "You just missed your friend," the girl said breathlessly. Her bicycle was propped against a tree on the green and she glanced at the windows of two cottages, noting with satisfaction that the curtains moved while she was talking to the famous model as if she really knew her.

"Missed who?" Paul's voice was sharp. "Were you expecting a visitor other than the cat you adopted?" he asked Catrina, trying to sound amused, and Catrina wondered if he disbelieved her story that she was alone in the cottage all last night.

"I was cycling along the lane delivering the parish magazine and thought you might like one; not that Carol ever bothers much but we do like to be friendly. And I saw this man coming from the back of the cottage as if he was trying to make someone hear. Such a good-looking man," she added.

"You mean my agent Max? You do know what he looks like, don't you?"

"No, I mean the man who did that very entertaining introduction to the fashion show at the manor. But of course you didn't see him that afternoon as you wanted to slip in quietly." Catrina stood quite still and Paul took her hand. "He didn't know me, of course, and I didn't say I knew who he was. I just called out that everyone from the cottage was out." She smiled, delighting in the knowledge that she was on friendly terms with Catrina and had recognised another celebrity. "I almost missed him. I had left my bike by the grass verge and was walking up to the front door with the magazine when he came from the back and looked very surprised to see me."

"What happened?"

Serena looked at Paul, surprised by his stern expression. "Nothing happened. He was rather silly. If he had waited I could have told him that Carol was away and you were staying here for a few days, and that you had only gone out for a walk with your friend. He could have waited for you in the village, as anyone walking over the hill usually comes back that way, but he pulled his scarf over his face as if he didn't want me to see him close up, almost ran to his car and drove away without a word." She looked mildly offended, then smiled. "I think now that I was mistaken and he may have sinus trouble. The winds here can be biting, as I know only too well. My father suffers when he has a funeral service in the open."

"How did you know I was out?"

"The postman saw you both walking up on the hill and Miss Randolph noticed that you had an early morning visitor." She looked at the telephone box. "Is your phone out of order? Do come to the vicarage and use ours if you are in any difficulty."

Paul's hand urged Catrina away. "As we've missed him we'll get back to the cottage, but if you see anyone else looking for us, be nice and phone, will you? We may or may not be going out again and it would give us . . . due warning to put the kettle on." He smiled and Serena blushed. "Come on, Catty. You have a few calls to make and I'm hungry so we'll eat at the cottage."

Catrina unlocked the front door and Paul went round the outside of the cottage to see if a forced entry had been tried but found that all the windows were still secure; so Giorgio hadn't managed to get inside the cottage. Catrina rang the police station number that the sergeant had given her and the receiver was lifted as if he was waiting for her call. She told him what had happened.

"You went out alone?" he snapped.

"No, Paul was with me. He came as soon as you called him."

"Keep him there."

"What did he say?" Paul asked.

"The nice sergeant says I have to keep you here with me. He seems to think I shall be safe with you." She smiled, mocking him, knowing that she was safe from serious personal subjects until the policeman had gone. Only unimportant subjects like murder now, she thought sadly.

Paul wandered outside the cottage again, taking care to keep to the paths but examining the flowerbeds and borders and when Sergeant Richmond arrived, he was able to show him a patch of earth disturbed underneath a back window, and a blurred shoeprint.

The sergeant bent down and looked at it closely. "You're sure that it was our friend?" he asked.

"The vicar's daughter has eyes like lasers and we saw a car like his waiting at the lights and pointing away from the village while we were on the hill. I didn't think it could be his car but Catrina was adamant, as usual. Surely he must be mad to come here?"

"Could be just that." Sergeant Richmond looked deadly serious. "We're beginning to think we may be dealing with someone who isn't normal, and the danger with people like that is that they are convinced that they are smarter than the police and do things that a normal criminal would avoid. Returning quite openly to cover his tracks might be one of them."

"Has he been back to the hotel?"

"No, but one of my men searching the woods in the area where we found the body saw a man answering his description. He ran off when he saw my man but dropped two things, a garden fork and a shoe."

"But why?" Catrina sank back into a chair and looked up at the two men.

"We think he came back to bury the girl, and to put the missing shoe with her. He can't have looked at the local papers this morning. The dailies had a small paragraph low down which could easily be missed."

"And he called here on his way?" A sick coldness made her feel faint and Paul took her hand.

"You're freezing. I'll get some coffee. Better still, beef extract and brandy." She nodded. "Frightened?"

"No, it isn't that. It's the thought of that poor girl lying out there waiting to be buried. With only one shoe."

"I promise you that she has two shoes now and is as clean and safe as she'll ever be."

Surprised by his understanding, she smiled. "Thank you, Sergeant. Do they call you Gerald or Gerry?"

"Either, but I'm not really a little potty." He had said it often and she knew it.

"I know the feeling. I used to be called Catty."

"You still are."

"Sergeant Gerald, you are quite insufferable. How can your wife stand a man who knows everything?"

"She knows the score. She was in the force too."

"She's much too pretty." He looked pleased. "What happened? Did she give it all up for love?" Paul put down the tray and listened as if what the sergeant said might have some relevance to his own problem.

"There was the child." End of argument. The pretty WPC became a housewife. Catrina raised her eyebrows. "She does follow some of the cases," Gerald Richmond said lamely. "And she threatens to go back to work as soon as Kim is older."

"Threatens?"

He shifted uncomfortably. "Well, there's really no need for her to do it." It was a quick retort, as if the argument had been discussed recently and had left an open space of dissension.

"You'd rather have your socks darned, if anyone darns socks anymore." Her smile was sweet but Paul knew just how angry she could get when she looked like that. "She can fade away at the sink . . . be washed down the drain while you bring home the bacon?"

He looked uneasy. "We work together. There are things I do best and Wanda is a good mother and cook."

Catrina glanced at Paul, the corners of her mouth turning down. He'd said almost the same. They could be equal partners, but some partners were more equal than others, didn't someone say? The telephone rang and the sergeant took it. "Important?" she asked.

"The estate car has been found abandoned a few miles from here. It was hired from a place in Sheffield last month by a man giving a fictitious name and address, so our friend may make a habit of doing that, hiring a car and leaving it when the heat gets to him, then hiring another and so on. Hiring gives him more time than stealing outright, as it takes time for the authorities to try to check the address given and to realise he has done a runner."

"So what now?" Paul asked.

"Routine checks on hire car firms with a photofit to find him and a lot of leg-work for my lads."

Catrina sipped her broth and shuddered at the amount of brandy in it while Paul and Richmond drank coffee, but she was warmer now. "So if he comes back, I shall have no idea what car he will be using?"

"We'll leave someone on watch."

"No, I'd look out and be convinced it was Giorgio in any lurking car. If anyone stays it has to be inside." Now offer me a nice policewoman to sleep in the spare room, she prayed, glancing at Paul.

"It would have to be a WPC," the sergeant said, before Paul could suggest himself. "Not you, sir," he said firmly. "But if you could stay in the pub for a night it would be useful. You've seen this man before and can keep us informed if he comes into the pub or if we want you to bring anything to the cottage. It would appear natural if you walked up the garden path and knocked on the door, but a policeman would scare him away."

"Do you know, Sergeant Gerald, I'd rather like to have him scared away before he got to the cottage."

Richmond looked down into the pale troubled face and hated what he had to say. "We have to get him. More information has been received. He spent some time in psychiatric hospitals and has an unhealthy obsession for his dolls. He likes to manipulate them as if they were human and he might have tried to do the same with Patricia. After a very successful public appearance, he might feel that he's a world-beater with power over lovely girls just as he has power over his dolls."

"And the girls were dressed as dolls! They even acted like dolls. He might have seen Patricia on stage at rehearsal, or she may have explained what the girls would have to do after his part in the show. What about the other girls who took part? They may be in danger."

"We have them under wraps, and fortunately the white make-up was a good disguise." The grey eyes were serious. "But he also saw you, Miss Catrina, so no answering the door to anyone who fails to produce identification, no going out alone and no visitors without clearing it with me, in case we make a mistake!"

"If you are going to tell me off, Sergeant Gerald, then please call me Catrina." He blushed. "Your Wanda wouldn't mind, would she?"

"I put too much brandy in that," Paul said and took away her mug. She glared at him. "I'll go down to the village now and get in some supplies for a couple of days. You have enough butter and milk but we need bread and eggs and a few extras like lean steak and chicken and fresh vegetables."

"I'd like to go too. I love the village shops. It isn't fair," she said but the brandy was losing its strength and she was almost glad to be organised. "Cancel all deliveries," she reminded him. "I don't want anyone coming to the door in vans or milk floats."

Paul drove away and Catrina made more coffee. "I would be quite all right alone if Paul was at the pub and you gave me all those phone numbers."

"No way," Richmond said. "Your fiancé will stay with you here until eleven and then I or one of my WPC's will take over, having walked from the village."

"My what?"

"He told me he wants to marry you and take you away for a rest."

"For the rest of my life?" She smiled, holding out her left hand. "No ring from earl or commoner, Sergeant, and I have no plans to mend socks."

"Don't you want marriage and a family?"

"Sometimes I think that it would be heaven, but that's

usually when I've had a tough day or have to fly to some awful place where the flies bite and the mineral water is never ice cold." She smiled. "Men like me, not just because of my looks, and I know that one day I shall have to give up much of my lifestyle and settle for a less public image." She turned away so that he couldn't read her eyes. "I've only really loved one man; well, maybe one and a half, but there are many others who would make me happy and secure and give me a good life and a fair amount of freedom to do what I need to do."

"What about the man you marry?"

"He'll get a loving wife and a good hostess and a mother for his children, if that's what he really wants from me."

"You make it sound clinical."

"I disagree. Some people leap into bed and have a passionate affair or get married on the crest of a wave of passion and then there is an anticlimax." She laughed. "Is that possible in sex? I can be more . . . generous, less selfish if I love a person slightly less than he loves me." She shrugged. "It must be the brandy making me drivel on like this. Good thing you are a tight-mouthed policeman and not a reporter or this would make the Sunday supplements."

"I'll check the locks and be away, but someone will be here at eleven tonight to stay until morning so that your friend can get some sleep at the pub and be here tomorrow, if needed. I think I hear his car now."

Catrina glanced over the net curtain that blurred the lower half of the window. "Yes, that's Paul. If Giorgio is watching, and I hope to God he isn't, he'll recognise that car – it sticks out like a sore thumb even in a crowded car-park."

Paul dumped the parcels on the kitchen table. "Any coffee?" he said, as if he hadn't tasted it for weeks.

"Of course. Fresh and hot," Catrina said, and Richmond grinned, told them to take care and went away to his very ordinary unmarked car.

"A few things for the freezer but the rest can wait," Paul said and poured coffee for two.

"Yes, sir! Paul, you have that look about you that says I'm either in disgrace or you have something to say that I will hate."

"And you aren't used to anyone saying anything to ruffle a hair of that wonderful head."

"I never liked being treated as a child of limited intelligence and it's a relief to be taken seriously by the very best in my profession," she said mildly.

"I'm not here to talk shop," he said impatiently.

"No, you're here to protect me and give me confidence," she said. "I could be in danger and if you try to bully me, I shall scream for a nice policeman to take your place."

"Bully you?" His expression made her laugh. "I never could bully you, Catty. It was you who got your own way most of the time."

"You went away and didn't write."

"You left first and made me see that we had no future together and drove me away to try to forget you."

"And we both prospered, as they say in books."

"Yes, we did, didn't we?" He gave a reluctant grin. "I suppose anger and frustration and an attitude of 'I'll show her!' have been valuable goads, but now I have made it and we can forget that we ever drifted apart."

"To do what, Paul?" She slipped away as he reached for her hand and he found himself holding a packet of frozen vegetables. "Better get them stacked," she said, and opened the door to the small freezer.

"Oh, Catty!" he said, rubbing his cold wet hand on his jacket, and they both laughed. He held her close, and she felt the deep throb of his heart as if it came from her own as he kissed her softly, experimentally, as if she might even now slap him down. "Where did you go?" he whispered. "I've missed you so much." His mouth was hungrier now, more urgent and his hands caressed her body and held her so that she knew his hardening desire. "You know you belong to me," he said, and his eyes were triumphant as her whole body softened.

She wanted to drown in the remembered love she had felt for him over the years but she drew back, the dregs of bitterness still there, the sense that this was what he wanted, to make her his, in an unequal union. A quick tumble would solve nothing except to make her feel cheap and put Paul firmly in command, and she had other matters on her mind just now, like a girl under damp bracken and a man who had called on her with a spade and a missing shoe.

"Can you say that you don't love me?" It was not a question, but a challenge to make her admit that she loved him above all other men.

"You're pushing me, Paul. Can't you see that this is no time for sex?" Deliberately she used the word. I love you, she wanted to say. I love you as I never thought I'd love anyone since I left for London all that time ago, when my heart was numb with pain and the thought that you could let me go and never write. If I once say it now before I am ready and you know I mean it, I am lost and my independence goes.

She could almost hear Sym's cynical voice and see Louis being tragic over the fact that he might lose his favourite model – he had no flair for designing maternity wear. She gave an involuntary giggle. "What's so funny?" Paul was puzzled and looked hurt.

"I think I need more coffee," she said. "What did you put in that Bovril?"

"That was ages ago. It's worn off by now."

"So I think I need some more in my coffee."

"Oh, no! You can't wriggle away on cloud nine when I have to talk to you seriously."

"Seriously, with no quick grabs at me to make me dissolve into a jelly?" She laughed. "It nearly worked, but there are a hundred things to discuss before we could ever be together, Paul."

He re-filled his coffee mug and found a cake tin on the dresser. "Like earls and castles and diamonds and marriage contracts?"

"That has been suggested," she admitted. "Also, I am at the height of my career but may not have much longer, so I want to enjoy it and not feel that I have to be with anyone anywhere unless I want it, and I haven't time to be pulled in two different directions, certainly not if one is the other side of the Atlantic."

"Or your agent tells you what you think you want to do." Paul's derision was the armour she needed.

"You would rather I took instruction in all things from you?"

"If you like." His mouth had the stubborn line that she had once slapped hard when he got too overbearing over a trip to the Cotswolds on a cold day, when he had wanted to take her with him on his old motorcycle and she had other plans for that weekend; but he wouldn't remember that.

"I don't like," she said. "There's a lot to be said for a man who is gentle with me and loves me with unquestioning tenderness and never says what he can give me, but lays it before me nevertheless and hopes I may pick it up. He is willing to let me do anything I like to further my career if I marry him, but he would shun the public side and let me still be Catrina."

"An aristocratic wimp!"

"That is what he is not. He doesn't have to prove anything by being macho and he has the sense to know that his gentle concern makes me gentle, too. I do love him in many ways, Paul, and he would care for me whatever I did."

"I care for you. Hell, Catty, I've loved you all my life!"

"I know. You love me but you don't want a real partnership. You want me as a wife who bends to her husband's wishes and smiles a lot while she does so. Poor Wanda."

"Who is Wanda?" Paul asked and sighed. "Here we go again. If you must sidetrack me, then do it with food, woman. I'm starving. Besides, I never knew a Wanda."

"Nor did I. Steak or fish?"

"Steak. Carol has a pressure cooker so we can have potatoes and mashed carrots."

"If you peel the potatoes," Catrina said. "They stain my fingers. Do plenty and put some in cold water for later."

"Later? Are you entertaining?"

"Only Sergeant Richmond, I think. Policemen are always hungry, so they say, but of course it might be a policewoman who sits in with me tonight."

"He can peel his own. You don't fancy him?"

Catrina shook her head. "No, and that's part of his charm. I like him, really like him, and know that he likes me, but we don't spark each other in that way or it might be tricky being alone with him." She put vegetable fat in the pan and sizzled an onion before searing the steaks and testing them for tenderness. "They'll be fine rare if that's what you want," she said.

Paul uncorked a bottle of red wine and nodded when Catrina went into the fridge for mineral water. "Better stay sober for your bit of rough trade," he said and grinned. "And don't give him this or you may have a surprise. If you believe that he doesn't fancy you rotten, you must be out of your mind."

Catrina turned the steaks and glared at him. "He is not rough trade and he likes me," she said, sending a spray of hot fat over the stove. "I'd trust him with my life." She shivered as if she saw it happening. If Giorgio came, would the sergeant carry a gun?

"No, not the news," Catrina said, when Paul went to switch on the radio. "I'd rather wait until we hear what real news there is and besides, I like to hear what's happening outside so I don't want radio or television just now."

Elizabeth Daish

"You really are worried."

"Well, wouldn't you be if a monster was after you?"

"Don't worry. You're in good hands and at last the police are taking you seriously," he said, as if he had battled with them for weeks to see reason.

"And *you* are taking it seriously and not saying that I'm an absolute idiot," she said. "That makes a change."

"Cool it, Catty. I'm sorry about that and you know I care a lot that you must be protected."

"Even by the sergeant?"

"I don't consider him a threat and he does know his stuff," he said slowly. "I also think you might take more notice of his warnings than if I tried to tell you what to do."

Catrina smiled infuriatingly. "It depends on what you tell me to do," she said. "And if you say please."

As they relaxed after their meal, footsteps reached the back door and Paul squinted through the frosted glass panel of the back porch. He unlocked the door for the sergeant. "You're early," he said resentfully.

"No point in keeping you from your sleep, sir, and my wife gets edgy if I'm moving about downstairs, waiting to go out when she's trying to sleep. She's had quite a day and needs her beauty sleep." He grinned. "I shall expect miracles when she has the new make-up, or I'll want my money back."

"From what I saw, she's half-way there without make-up." Catrina smiled with genuine warmth. "She's really pretty and if your little girl takes after her, you'll have a load of trouble when she gets bigger, or will she be a big butch policewoman, taking after her father?"

"She's like Wanda," Richmond said, and Paul felt excluded. Catrina had been relieved when the sergeant arrived, relaxing visibly as soon as she saw him, as if he made her forget the tragic events that brought them together instead of making her more conscious of the murderer who might be waiting somewhere out in the darkness.

"I could have stayed here all night," Paul said. "Surely a policeman of your rank must have more pressing duties. I thought there was a manpower shortage in the force."

"We are very grateful for your help, sir, and it's good to know that you are on call at the pub, but I have a radio and can contact my men quickly if needed."

Catrina saw the satisfied glint in the sergeant's eyes. No way would he willingly give up this onerous stint, protecting a pretty woman and making him the envy of the station. "Does Wanda sleep easily knowing that you are here on duty?" she asked.

"She thinks I'm in charge of operations from the van parked in the wood with a link to the station," he said calmly. "But I thought you'd rather have someone here who you knew and not a complete stranger."

"That was kind," she said, mocking him. "I suppose you'll soon be hungry again, too?"

"I can see that I am quite superfluous," Paul said. He collected his coat and his briefcase and made for the front door.

"Yes, go ride your bike, Paul, but don't go away. I do need you around."

"If that much has registered, I'm making progress. Remember, if you need me tonight, I can be here in minutes. I had a word with the landlord, told him I might have to ride over rough ground and he offered me the bike his son had when he left the army. It's a good machine and I turned it a bit and oiled it. I can come over the field there and in through the back door quietly and very quickly."

She followed him to the door, lifting her face for his kiss, and clinging to him for a moment. "Paul, darling, I do love you."

His mouth was hard and angry on hers. "Do I have to wait until you are old and ugly before you will come to me, Catty? Do I have to wish away the good years before you will want me? Oh, Catty, I want you so much."

"Come tomorrow, and we'll walk the hill again." She watched him go and heard the powerful engine of the American car that would convince anyone watching that he was really leaving, then went back to the kitchen where the kettle was boiling fast and Sergeant Richmond was standing looking vaguely helpless.

"It boiled," he said.

"It does that," she agreed. "Coffee and an omelette suit you?"

"I wonder you haven't been voted the the most unpopular woman of the year by the feminist vote. It's not really fair that you should look as you do and be a dream of a cook, too."

"Really, Segeant Gerald, I had no idea that you were permitted to make such observations."

He grinned. "Part of the training to notice every detail."

If it wasn't for the undercurrent of anxiety that she felt, this could be fun. For so long, Catrina had been feted by people who took her too seriously, and this friendly banter made her recall girls and boys she had once known, growing up, who teased and said what they thought and laughed a lot. She smiled. Paul still hankered after dirty motorbikes. He must have been delighted to be shown a badly-kept old ruin that he could soothe back to smooth working condition, and she wondered if he would buy it to add to his garage collection.

Perhaps there were two crash helmets and they could ride together again, his words whipping past her in the wind and her arms locked round his body. "Do you ride a motorcycle, Sergeant?" she asked.

"I did." His face was suddenly lined, a young-old face remembering. "Wanda made me give it up after something happened. We weren't married then but it was on the cards and a cycle rider is very vulnerable."

"You had an accident?"

"We were chasing a villain and he was armed." He glanced at her and grinned. "Not to worry, we got him and I had only a flesh wound."

"And now you have to wear a bathing costume with sleeves, or long legs or whatever?" He obviously wanted to keep it light, so she smiled, and he relaxed again, but she had glimpsed the underlying resentment that he was no longer allowed to prove that particular lack of fear.

"Something like that." So Wanda had given up her job, and he had given up a masculine joy for her. It helped. What would Paul give up for her? Liberty, certainly. Now, he could go where he wanted, take any woman he fancied if he desired her enough and have the best of all worlds. Women would take any chance they could to meet him, making sex easy. He had matured into the kind of man that most women dreamed of waking up next to.

"One cheese omelette coming up," she said.

"I'll just check the security first," Sergeant Richmond said.

Seven

Catrina doodled on a sketch pad as they drank the last of the coffee. She changed a line here and there and a design emerged.

"That's very good. Is there no end to your talents?" Sergeant Richmond looked over her shoulder on his way to the kitchen with the loaded tray.

"Leave all that," she said and yawned. "We can do it in the morning. Carol should get a dishwasher. It's midnight and I'm tired."

"It will give me something to do," he said. He backed into the kitchen door to open it, then turned with the tray and put it on the draining board, nearly spilling the cream, as the telephone suddenly shrilled.

Catrina beat him to it. "It's most likely for me," she said. "Max or Sym always ring at ungodly hours. I sometimes think they're trying to check on me to make sure I haven't a lover." Richmond shook his head, thinking that it must be for him and cursing whoever disturbed Catrina at this hour. He had stressed that he would do the calling unless his lot used radio with something vital to tell him, but she backed away and lifted the receiver. "Sorry about that if it's my DC," Richmond said. "I said

I'd check with the van later but they may have something fresh for me."

"Arbutus Cottage," Catrina said.

"Catrina?" The voice was masculine and deep.

"Who are you?" She glanced at the sergeant and raised her eyebrows as if puzzled.

"Forgive me for ringing so late, but I find that I am in the district tomorrow. Symfony told me that you were in the cottage and where to find it, and I wondered if you could spare me ten minutes of your time for a couple of country shots. I'm Robert Henning. You worked with me some time ago. Remember the spread in *Good Housekeeping*?"

"Robert Henning? Yes, of course I remember, but I thought you left for America."

"So I did for a time but I'm back for a while. I do want those pictures if it's possible. I could be company for you, too. I assume that you are there alone?"

"Quite alone, as I thought I was to have a well-earned rest. Max does all my bookings, so you should really contact him. I'm having lunch with someone tomorrow but I could see you during the afternoon. I'll meet you by the church, and meanwhile please try to get Max and tell him what is happening."

"No, not the village. I'll pick you up at the cottage."

"But I haven't brought any gear with me that you would want in a picture."

"You'll be fine in jeans and sweater and maybe a dog? It's for a 'Come to the Country' sort of travel thing."

"No dog, I'm afraid." Catrina said.

"No dog? Well, it can't be helped." She thought he

138

sounded not too disappointed. She frowned and the sergeant watched her closely.

"Shall we say three o'clock in the afternoon and you'll try to get Max before then?"

"That will suit me very well," he said.

She replaced the set on the table and frowned. The sergeant watched her. "Something wrong?"

"I'm not sure. You'll say that I'm imagining things, as you did when you thought I hadn't seen a body in the car."

He shook his head and sat on the arm of her chair, his eyes hard. "Go on, tell me. Who is Robert Henning?"

"I worked with him about two years ago. He's a very good photographer and nobody turns him down unless they have a very good reason. Everyone wants to work with him but he spends most of his time in Miami now and Sym nearly spits blood when she sees his work over there, using none of her creations. I said I'd meet him here because it would have seemed very odd if I had turned him down, even when I am on holiday."

"So what's wrong?"

"Robert, unless he has a very bad cold, or has undergone a virility change, had a voice that is light and rather precious, with lots of darlings and sweeties in every sentence. This voice was dark and low and what do you think? No middle European gentleman should attempt words like Henning or any word with H in it." She was pale now.

The sergeant took her cold hand in his. "You were wonderful. You even convinced me that he was bona."

It was comforting and she smiled. "Does that mean you'll have a posse waiting tomorrow afternoon?"

"No white horses and six-guns, but something like that. At least we can surround the area and post men at every approach road."

"You will check every car that comes into the village?"

He hesitated, his glance flickering away from her anxious stare. "Not exactly. If he saw the road blocked, he would do a U turn and get away up the motorway and off."

"What if you miss him? He has changed his car by now."

"Someone will be here. You keep your lunch date as if nothing is wrong and come back here with your fiancé at about two thirty, unlocking the door as if the cottage is empty, and saying goodbye on the doorstep. We shall be inside, and by then we shall know how he is travelling and what he's wearing. He can't get away this time."

"Don't go away." Catrina smiled wanly and went to her room. She looked out over the forsythia bush nodding by the hedge and wished that there was less cover for anyone trying to approach the cottage. She tried to read for a while in bed, but the rustling outside kept her awake. She knew that the shadows on the walls were not witches or murderers but her book failed to grip her. She could hear the faint but solid sound of Sergeant Richmond talking on his radio and she knew she was safe.

She slipped into sleep, dreaming of Paul, looking fierce. He said he would never let her out of his life again and she believed him. I want that, too, she decided. It isn't worth the hassle to stand up for my independence. I can't lose him now.

She turned over in bed and knocked the alarm clock to the floor, and was suddenly wide awake. She heard the whine of the milk-float coming from the village and remembered that Richmond had wanted everything to seem normal, but said that the float would be watched from a distance as it left the village. It was a grey morning and a cool breeze stirred the bushes. A bird with a bizarre idea of entertainment made a frantic noise outside her window and she realised it was the alarm call of a blackbird. "That tabby tom," she said softly. "What ingratitude after I fed you milk yesterday."

She sorted out clothes for the day and made as little noise as possible. With any luck, the sergeant was getting some sleep on the settee in the sitting room downstairs, and she hoped that he would have enough rest to keep him on the ball later when he was needed.

The shower room was away from the sitting room end of the cottage and she knew she could use it without disturbing him, so she stripped and took her time over a shower, revelling in the hot sharp spray and the scented steam.

As if preparing for a show, she smoothed her skin with lotion and tidied her nails, patted her face with skin freshener and plucked two hairs from her eyebrows. It was routine and without it she would have felt half-dressed and not quite clean. The bathroom window rattled and she wondered if it might be chilly outside, so she dressed warmly in a thick sweater and velvet jodhpurs that could be worn with boots later if she went walking with Paul. It was comfortable and chic and she twisted her hair into a sleek knot and found a scarf that matched her eyes.

She stared at her reflection. I look quite normal, she thought. Ready for a casual breakfast and lunch date with the man I want to marry, but later, much later. It was still very early. Down in the garden, a flurry of scared feathers made her look down. The cat was poised, pale yellow eyes intent on something just out of her view. The bird scolded again and flew up, the cat after it, missing by inches. The bird trailed a wing as if injured, to tempt the cat away fron the nest high in the bush, and the cat waited.

Catrina hurried downstairs softly. If I give him some milk, it will allow the bird to take cover, she thought. The milk-van had stopped whining up the hill and she couldn't remember hearing the man leave the two pints of milk for the cottage, but she had been in the shower and might have missed him. Would the sergeant want cornflakes for breakfast?

The cat yowled again at the back door. "You can wait," she whispered. Cunning with it, she decided. He knew that the dogs were away and he could scrounge milk as soon as the milkman arrived. She took a saucer from the sitting room sideboard on her way to the kitchen and paused to look at the sleeping face against the chintzy cushions.

Lucky Wanda, she thought. A good face; stubborn but that had to be in his job. Honest and a mouth that was satisfyingly sensual with no excesses. His hair grew into a peak on his forehead and his eyes were sunken with the fatigue he would never admit to when awake. He was deeply asleep and she crept past him, glad that her walking shoes were rubber-soled. The milk in the fridge was still fresh and she tipped half a bottle into a saucepan, as she decided to make hot chocolate. She lit the gas and filled the saucer with milk. The yowling began again only louder and on a more urgent note. What a noise for one small animal.

She unbolted the back door, slid back the safety chain and unlocked the main Chub, as secure as the Bank of England, and bent to put the saucer on the uneven stone step, intent on not spilling any.

Cats! Even they must read my publicity blurbs, she thought. The feature with seven Siamese cats draped over a velvet couch was best forgotten. After that, she had received offers of thirty-four kittens as she was so obviously a cat lover!

A shadow fell across the steps but it was no tomcat. She turned but a hand over her mouth and another pushing her arm high behind her back made struggling impossible. The pain was intense and she wondered how far the tension could go before something snapped. The door swung and she hoped it made a noise. This was ridiculous. In there was a hefty police detective sergeant who was protecting her! The heels of her shoes left furrows in the soft turf as she was dragged away from the cottage. The man was very strong and knew exactly where he was going.

From the edge of her vision she saw the derelict shed with its door hanging away from the hinges. There were men gathering at every crossroads, in every farmyard and track and in the sliproads of the motorway, watching and waiting. The police of seven counties were looking for him but they had overlooked the old shed in the cottage orchard as he was expected to arrive much later. The timing had been wrong. He must have brought the van she now saw in the shed as soon as he ditched the estate car and left it there, walking unseen among the bushes to make his call from the telephone situated behind the church, among greenery that made it less conspicuous in the pretty village.

He knew that there was no dog to give the alarm and that she would take in the milk. The cat calls were hammed up but convincing and the gap between the cottage and the bushes was narrow. The bend in the lane hid them from sight in seconds. Catrina struggled and tried to be a dead weight to make him pause but the relentless fingers clamped harder and his rings cut into her mouth, making her taste blood. The nightmare was reality.

The rear doors of the van were open and Catrina was thrust inside. She collided with a heavy packing case and sank to the floor as he released her. She gasped for breath as she was half-suffocated and then tried to stand. She faced him. "Why me?" she asked.

He slapped her face. "You will be very quiet. Dolls talk when I say and not before." He smiled and she wondered how she could ever have thought him sane. "Patricia talked out of turn and had to be punished, so keep quiet until I find out if you were telling me the truth last night on the telephone."

"There's nobody in the cottage," she lied, hoping desperately that Richmond had heard them. Her hand was wet and she recalled that the milk had slopped over it when Giorgio grabbed her. Milk! The milk on the stove must have boiled over by now. She tensed, listening and thought she heard footsteps. She moved her feet to mask the sound. Let it be him, she prayed. Let him come to me. "I'm expecting a visitor this morning," she said, hoping that he would think she was lying. "My fiancé is coming to breakfast and he'll find me gone." In the distance she heard a motorcycle engine cough and stop. Hurry, Paul! Oh, please make the bloody thing go, and hurry! her mind screamed.

"I said that dolls talk when I say." The rag he stuffed into her mouth was stale as if it had been in a deep trunk for years and the cords on her wrists were harsh and made her stop moving. The door slammed shut and he shot the outside bolt home. Catrina wriggled to look over the edge of the packing case and saw that there were windows in the van, but even if her mouth was free she knew that no one would hear her if she shouted for help.

A neatly folded rug made her shudder and the black, coffin-like case that held his dolls was a sharp reminder of dolls mute or dead. This was an old van but sturdily built and one that the villagers would not notice in passing. He could have bought it cheaply from a corner site selling used cars, paying cash with no questions asked and a false address. The locals would have thought it belonged to a farmer or to a rep travelling in farm goods or fodder. There had been a few vans parked on a grass verge, belonging to travellers selling junk and totting for old clothes outside the village, and even the curtain twitchers had no interest in them apart from making sure that the council turned them away at the earliest opportunity.

She listened again. His voice sounded sharply, threatening and low and two sets of footsteps came across the rough lane. The door jerked open and Detective Sergeant Richmond was pushed inside, the door shut and bolted again and Giorgio's face appeared at one of the windows.

He smiled. "So you were alone last night!" Richmond pushed at the door but it was firm. "Quiet, my friend. If you try that then the little doll must go." Catrina saw the glint of a knife and then the face at the window disappeared.

Richmond was silent and grim, taking the gag from her mouth and the cords from her wrists and ankles. "Did he take you by surprise too?" she asked.

"Not altogether but he had a knife and I was afraid for you." He dabbed tenderly at her bruised lips with a clean tissue. "I had to know where you were, so I went along with him. Thank heaven for the milk boiling over on the stove. I was awake and in the kitchen when he came back and tapped on the door. I thought it was you and was ready to tell you what a fool you were to venture out alone, and then I saw the knife and thanked God that as yet there was no blood on it." He touched the bruised cheek with care. "You'll have a shiner tomorrow," he said cheerfully.

"You could have escaped," she said in wonder.

"No, I had to get to you quickly and I had no idea where to look among the bushes. I saw the marks on the turf where he dragged you and thought . . ."

"You thought he had strangled me as he did Patricia?"

He shrugged. "Even a gag can suffocate a helpless victim," he said mildly. "And you weren't screaming."

"You could have stayed and rung the others to help you search. I'm not worth a valuable officer risking his life."

"I was there to protect you and I failed. I saw your tracks as we went up the lane and was really worried. Now I am here and he'll get to you over my dead body, but for Christ's sake never ever feed tomcats again."

She managed a shaky smile. "Your Wanda is a very lucky woman, Gerald." He blushed and moved away to the window. "We're moving," she said. "What do we do now?"

"Ride," he said with a faint smile. "While I talk to the lads." He took a small transmitter from his back pocket. "I thought it was crushed but it seems to work." He spoke quietly and briefly and grinned. "Thank God they're on the ball. I don't think he can hear anything while the engine revs like that. It's hardly a getaway car!"

The van wheezed along the narrow lane away from the village and on to the rough ground above the back of the cottage. "Where the hell is he going?" The engine coughed and accelerated, the wheels churning the early celandines and the soft turf. "He'll be lucky to get to the top and over the other side," he said.

"He may just be looking for somewhere to hide," Catrina said. "Maybe he'll leave us in the van and get away on foot." The van lurched and rocked over the ground where she had walked with Paul. How odd, she thought. I may not come out alive and yet this is the place where I had planned to tell Paul that I would marry him. She saw the bright flash of gorse, young on the bushes, and the silver and grey-blue of the morning sky. All the signs of new growth and fresh life were there. It was spring and she might leave nothing behind but a lot of outdated magazine fashions and a few portraits that would drift into people's nostalgic memories.

She looked at the sergeant and wondered how any woman could marry a policeman and have children from choice. He might die with her in the van and Wanda would be left with Kim, a child that Catrina would never meet but must look a little like him. I'm not worth the effort and the danger, she decided. If he could crash the door open, she would stay as hostage or victim to let him escape back to his wife and child and she hoped that he'd have the sense to do so, but as she gazed at his set face, she was humbled by his care and her tears were not for herself.

The van stopped and quivered until the engine was killed. The driver's door opened and the two in the back tried to see what Giorgio was doing. Catrina climbed on to the long black box to get to the other window as Giorgio walked round the van. The box collapsed, revealing one of the dolls. It was the doll dressed in Louis's creation, the vivid skirt making a rainbow of colour against the dull wood. Catrina dragged another small box to the window and climbed on to it, propping up the doll at one side so that she wouldn't trip over it when she slid back to the floor.

Richmond had his face close to the window on his side and Giorgio saw him. The man laughed and shook a large canister so that he could hear liquid swishing inside. "Christ almighty! He's mad. He's going to burn the van," Richmond said and spoke again into the radio, then went to the other window where Giorgio appeared without the canister. He peered into the back of the van at the doll and his face was contorted with something like grief. The doll sat on the remains of the case, hands folded and face white and expressionless as the girls had been at the fashion show.

Catrina arranged the doll's skirts to a wide arc of colour. "If you burn us, you burn Gloria," she said, recalling the name of the doll he had used in the cabaret at the Ragged Bear. He stared, in an agony of indecision and Catrina smoothed the false hair and touched the hands of the doll as if she found it beautiful. Giorgio seemed to be riveted to the ground.

"Of course," Richmond said. "To him the dolls are real. They are his women." He pushed Catrina to one side and took the doll in his arms. He kissed the blank face and glanced out at the stricken man, who clenched his fists in anger and frustration. "How much for a bit of business, you stupid bitch?" he said, coarsely and very clearly. He deliberately fondled the stuffed body and put a hand up inside the skirt, making obscene remarks that he hoped that Catrina had either heard and dismissed as the norm for rough men like policemen or if she didn't know them would not understand what they meant.

Giorgio was furious. He pounded at the window, demanding that Richmond must stop. The insult to his beautiful companion was more than he could bear. Catrina joined in, tearing the shirt to expose the padded bra under it. She ripped the skirt and Richmond pushed the doll to the floor of the van, out of sight of the man at the window.

"Promise you'll never tell a soul! Wanda would kill me," Richmond said. "I hardly ever rape ventriloquists' dolls, and this one is definitely not my type." He sat on the doll and Catrina bent over them to hide them from the man's desperate gaze.

There was silence and Catrina peeped out of the window. "He's searching for the keys. I saw him throw them away when he stopped the van so that we would have no means of escape through the cab doors, but I don't think he locked the back, he only slid the bolt across, but he's forgotten that now in his panic."

"He's looking on the wrong side of the van. They're over there," Richmond said. "I've told my back-up where to look, but I think he's sure to open up to rescue his precious Gloria or whatever he calls this one."

"What do we do if he unlocks the van? Rush him?" Catrina's eyes gleamed.

"You've been watching too much telly." Richmond looked under the rugs and beyond the boxes. "Leave it to me and the lads, but first I must have something to use when he comes at me with that knife." He lifted the skirt of the doll. "Pardon me, madam," he said, wrenching off one leg. "Sarah Bernhardt managed with one."

"She'll have to manage with none. Give me the other one," Catrina demanded.

"You stay out of this."

"Rubbish. If he comes with a knife, you'll want a diversion and he can't get both of us at once. I can't stay here doing nothing, sergeant dear; this is no time for me to look beautiful and hope for deliverance. I was a vicious hockey player, and have very strong wrists." He grinned and tore away the other leg, then propped the torso up against the window with the white face to the glass.

The canister of gasolene lay on its side, the fuel seeping out on to the ground and the smell penetrating the van. "Let's hope he doesn't fancy a quick drag and light a match," Richmond said casually, but the pulse in his temple showed great tension. "Come on, think! You don't need the keys; just lift the bar and let me get at you." He stopped. "Did you hear that?"

They held their breath and the sound came again. A high-powered motorcycle was coming along the lower lane and another less powerful one from the top of the hill. The sounds died and Richmond grunted his satisfaction. The man outside had not heard the engines.

"I think one was Paul," Catrina said.

"And one of ours, most certainly, and keeping a low profile until they get the order to rush the van. Oh, *no!*" Another sound came from the distance. It might have been an ambulance about its normal duties, but it sounded like a police car. At least Giorgio must have thought so as he listened. He seized a piece of wood with which to attack the windows, but the glass was shockproof and very thick and the wood bounced off. Furious again, he caught up the canister and a rainbow of oil covered the window. He ran round the van, splashing more and more gasolene and listened again but now there was silence.

"Get back," he called to the gorse bushes and the empty hillside. "If anyone comes I light a match." He searched again and found the keys. He gave a cry of triumph. He fumbled with the lock of the door and found that it was already open then tried to lift the bar across the double loading doors at the back. He stopped, the door still fast under the bar. "Go away," he called. "Go away or they die."

The knife was in his hand. "Keep back in there and give me my Gloria," he shouted. Behind him a movement came from the hill.

"You can't get away. All the roads are blocked," Richmond yelled. "You know you can't make it so why kill more innocent people?" Giorgio ran to the front of the

151

van and unlocked the door. The engine started then died and Richmond kicked the van sides and yelled. "Scream as loud as you can," he ordered. "They are rushing him and he's spotted them. If this thing goes up, lie on the floor with your head covered." The engine refused to start again, then a spark caught the fuel in the air and Giorgio jumped from the cab and came again to the window. Richmond seized the thick rug and wound it round Catrina's head and shoulders.

Beyond the window came a second red dawn, but of fire. The flames seemed to explode with rage as the breeze caught the burning oil. Heat came into the van from the blazing cabin and the smell of burning rubber mingled with melting plastic as the doll by the window slowly disintegrated into a mess of sad droplets. Giorgio saw it happening and ran to the window, his arms outstretched and tears running down his cheeks. The breeze took a turn and licked round his splashed clothes. He flung himself to the ground, enveloped in flames and Catrina tried to breathe through the thick blanket.

The door rattled and was flung wide. In a haze, Catrina heard police sirens and ambulance bells and men shouting as Sergeant Richmond seized the rug and pulled her out of the van, somersaulting and dragging her after him as the inrush of air blasted the flames into deadly life. He caught her up in his arms and rolled in the grass to put out the flames, enveloping them until other hands came with wet blankets and pulled him away.

"Catrina!" Paul's face was a blur but not a dream,

and it receded into mist as he stepped back away from her, leaving only the memory of the horror he registered.

There seemed to be no point in staying conscious or even of living.

Eight

The dream wouldn't go away. Hot smoke and the sound of engines racing, windows exploding into showers of hot glass that made her face feel as if it was being cut by a thousand cruel blades and a doll breaking and dissolving in mute resignation. That made two dolls, the one at the window and the one rolling in flames on the cool wet grass.

A nurse came and closed the door. Did I scream? Catrina couldn't remember but the nurse looked mildly reproachful, as if pain was no excuse for bad manners. She took out her watch and made a note on a chart.

Two lumps of white padding slung in front of her had no relationship to her body. They didn't belong at all, and were just bundles of something wrapped in cotton wool. But then she had no body left. It had all dissolved, melted like the plastic doll and was left lying in a puddle on the hillside.

"Did they leave my shoes on?" she asked. "I hate the thought of dying without shoes." A sensation of stuffiness and lack of movement made her sure that she was made of cotton wool like the lumps strung up on slings. She breathed more deeply and her nose hurt with the effort.

154

She tried to look down but gave up when the skin at the side of her head and neck tightened. Was she wearing the white make-up that she had worn in the fashion show? But now it was on her neck and shoulders and all over. It was tight and surely unnecessary now.

Someone smelling of soap and pleasant talc eased a plastic tube between her lips. "That's better," a voice said when the fluid level in the feeder went down.

Catrina drank again and the room came into focus, but her voice was slow as if out of practice and in a whisper as if it needed air. "What happened?"

"There was an accident." The eyes held enquiry. How much did the patient remember?

"I feel stiff."

"You were burned and cut but you are getting better. One more drink and you must sleep again."

Her mind began to work. She was far too tired to argue but she needed one answer. "Sergeant Richmond?"

"He's going to be all right. He's in the next private room. You seemed to have him on your mind, but there's no need to call out for him now. He's safe and getting better. You kept saying that he isn't a little potty."

Catrina tried to smile but it wasn't a good idea. "And Giorgio?" Everything was coming back.

"Sergeant Richmond said that his clothes caught fire when he tried to reach the burning doll." The eyes flickered away.

"Where is he?" Catrina insisted.

"He died in the ambulance."

"Poor Giorgio; he caused a lot of bother."

"Sister said that you must sleep." The guilty expression

showed that she was a junior who had said too much and mentioned forbidden subjects, but she was too good to let go.

"What about my face?"

The hesitation was too long and the smile too bright and her lack of experience was revealing. "You had a very lucky escape. Now you must sleep. Are you comfortable?"

"Yes, thank you, Nurse." Was numbness comfort? Was a complete indifference to what might be in the future, comfort? Was the limbo of half-sleep under sedation, comfort? She drifted between sleep and wakening, and it didn't matter that her face might never turn men's heads again.

When the dressings were soaked away and pain came back, she didn't know if it was her own voice crying out, and she was terrified, but Sister had a merciful syringe and the world fell back again. She gave in to whatever they wanted from her and behaved well. The time for crying and maybe hysteria would come later when Paul came to look at her in pity or disgust.

The scent of flowers grew stronger each day as more and more people heard of her plight. Nurses sighed as they wheeled in trolleys of pot plants and magnificent bouquets that couldn't be put anywhere but on the floor.

"More flowers," Sister said and tried to look pleased.

"Let the nurses take some home and give the rest to the wards that have few flowers brought in," Catrina suggested. "I'll read the cards first and Nurse Johns is making a note of who sent them so that I can get them acknowledged later."

Some flowers she kept and was touched by. Sym sent her small posies which went well on the table and held stilted messages that showed a lot of sincerity. So Sym had a soft spot for her apart from the beauty bit.

Louis sent, too, and she couldn't look at his gift in case her heart broke. He sent a light, exquisite turban with streamers that could be arranged in any way she liked to hide the injuries. As if I could ever wear it, she thought. But they gave her no mirror and she couldn't tell what might be her future.

Paul sent stiff bouquets with cards written in the shop. She remembered him once, through her drugged sleep, but now he was only a remembered voice. The hands that touched her were professional and caring in an impersonal way, dressing the hurt that was skin deep but having no impact on the scars within.

The dressings came off her hands first, and she no longer had to watch them hanging in the padding. She could move her fingers and the grafted skin pulled less but they were still not really hers. She felt mummified but better. The flowers looked brighter and more lovely now and she examined the cards herself.

Paul came to visit again, explaining that he had gone back to the States as soon as he saw that she had every care, to give her time to recover, but he had looked at his watch and left after a very short time. To give me time to get used to being without him again, she thought.

"No more visitors," she told the doctor after Paul left.

"You are much better," the doctor said firmly. "You

should see your friends, but I promise that there will be no Press getting anywhere near you. We're good at that here."

"I don't need to see them. I can use the phone now that I have the use of my hands. If they come here, they can't see me through the dressings but I can see them and read what they think of all this. Don't you see how depressing that could be?"

"It isn't as bad as you think." But his eyes held a noncommittal expression as if he must say all the right things but knew them to be false. "We are keeping the face covered with cream to keep it moist and elastic but you will have that taken away soon." He sat on the bed and smiled. "You've had hundreds of calls and half the flowers in London and stacks of lovely gifts from your business contacts and colleagues. Don't you think you owe them something now?"

"No." She stared at him through the gaps in the dressings and he walked to the window and bent to read the card attached to a magnificent vase of flowers. The vase had come with the flowers and was priceless. "I owe them nothing, Doctor. They've taken enough from me to leave me with no sense of guilt. In my trade, a woman is only as good as her last picture, her last show. They have enough in the can of Catrina to last for a very long time. After that, will there be a Catrina left?" Tears began to soak the dressings again.

"What about your real friends?" He sat on the bed again and watched her eyes. "I hear that you are engaged."

She shook her head, and held out her left hand. It looked small and thin and shiny on the palm where the burns had been bad and the ringless fingers were slightly clawed. "Can you imagine a huge ring on that?"

She reached for a small box on the bedside table and opened it with difficulty. The sapphires and diamonds sparkled up at her. She put the ring on the index finger and waved it in the air, trying to smile but suddenly it hurt to swallow. She had been so sure that the earl would send a get well message and flowers and go away to one of his villas to forget her.

"So you *are* engaged!" She felt his relief. She was safely in someone's care and perhaps there would be no need for prolonged tranquillisation or a psychiatrist.

"No, I said I wouldn't marry him, but this came today with an invitation to convalesce on his yacht at Antibes and to marry him in Edinburgh in the New Year." She turned the ring to catch more light and then carefully put it away.

"You'll accept? I think I can say that you could go to Antibes with a nurse if you promised not to exert yourself too much or get too hot. Let me think. Six weeks from today should be about right. You will have the dressings off your face and the stitches removed from the grafts on your shoulders and back in three weeks time. The patches on your thigh where we took the skin for the pinch grafts has healed nicely." He looked more cheerful. "It will be something for you to keep your mind occupied. I'm afraid that there are still some fragments of glass in your face that will have to be done in a day or so, and we'd like to do that under local anaesthetic."

"First the good news and then the bad!" She knew that she was smiling under the dressings but he could see only her eyes. "And when do we have the grand unveiling? Do I see myself soon, or is it too bad yet?"

He made a note on her chart. "Soon," he told her. "It bruises each time we take out splinters and looks worse than it is and the side of your head that was burned will have to have another small graft behind the ear."

"I have an ear?" He looked at her sharply, taken off guard by her light mocking.

"You have two perfectly good ears and everything to make a basis for a good face, as soon as the inflammation has gone. You don't look bad now but I'd rather wait until the last of the splinters are out and the swelling has gone."

"How is your sewing? Do you ever drop a stitch, Doctor? And my hands?"

"If you do the exercises and we release the tendons making the fingers claw, you will have a hand as good as new except for a slight shininess on the palm." He picked up her left hand and compared it with the right, which was almost normal.

"I must be better. You are talking to me as if I have a mind." He blushed slightly. "I know it must be difficult," she said, gently. "But please tell me what to expect. I have had a long time with nothing to do but think and I can only accept what you say. Have I a future in my work? Can I ever walk down a catwalk and show my body, my legs, my face, my arms? Shall I lose the stiffness that makes me walk as if I am a hundred? If you were him," she said, pointing to the box containing the ring, "could you kiss me, make love to me, and be seen in public with me, without being ashamed or repulsed?"

160

"You have many friends. They really love you." She took her hands away. "Listen. They love the woman under the façade and at least you will know who are your friends."

"That doesn't answer my question, Doctor."

"He has telephoned every day, sometimes twice a day and I spoke to him two days ago." She sat still, pushing back against the slope of pillows. "He wanted to know when you will be able to travel. He didn't want to know how you would look. He told me quite bluntly that he wanted to hear no platitudes as he knows that you will be disfigured, and he wouldn't listen when I tried to tell him that you would look good." His voice took on a hard edge and he took her hands in his again. "Don't underestimate him, Catrina. I think he wants to look after you and he must love you very much."

"I could still give him pretty babies. Injuries and acquired ugliness are not hereditary." The bitterness was there again. "I know that my beauty attracted him and I can't believe that he can look far beyond that, whatever he says."

And yet, she thought, he is the one who has been faithful.

"Reception vets most of the calls and Sister the rest but I did speak personally to the earl, as he made it plain that he had a vested interest in you and hoped to marry you." Julian would, she thought. Generations of men demanding answers because they held rank and privilege made it easy for him to get what he wanted, even in these more egalitarian times. "By the way, the latest batch of mail is over there. Is there anyone you would like to see? You have to make the effort soon," the doctor said, quietly but firmly.

"I want to see one man. How is Sergeant Richmond?"

"Much better, beginning to grumble at his inaction and worrying about the price of this place."

"Tell him from me that he mustn't worry about any cost." She was surprised that Max had arranged it all so willingly and even after the first shock was over he had made no sign of objecting to her paying for the expensive private care for the sergeant. She smiled. "Maybe he'd rather be in a general ward with others, but I wanted him to have the very best and privacy when his wife visited him. I know he's more a beer man and quite unimpressed by champagne, but he must put up with it!"

"You can see him soon. When he was under traction, he couldn't come to you, and you certainly couldn't visit him, but he's coming off traction today and we'll trundle him along on a trolley or in a chair as soon as Sister thinks he can take it."

"How badly was he hurt, Doctor?"

"He was lucky. He came out of the van on a blast of air and missed some of the burning. He dragged you with him and your clothes were alight and then your hair. I'm afraid you caught most of the glass splinters too, and he'll be free to leave before you may go. He broke his right leg badly in the fall, had a cracked rib or two and one finger of his left hand, but the orthopaedic team got to his leg fast and that made all the difference to his recovery."

"Give him my love and invite him to tea," she said.

"He sent you this." She took the heavy marble egg from his hand and turned it over and over, smiling. The doctor saw the gleam in her eyes. "He said it's a worry stone and will be useful to have by you."

"Darling Sergeant Gerald," she said. She twisted her fingers to roll the egg in her palm.

"He's right. That's better than any exercise. It becomes compulsive and you won't know that you are using it soon. Put it in the left hand and show me what you can do."

"It's a conspiracy," she said, but her spirits lifted as her hand began to ache.

"Five minutes at a time, many times a day, increasing daily," he said and left her to play with her toy. She can't be in love with the policeman, he thought, but knew that there must be some man who should be asking questions and was killing her with his silence.

Catrina glanced through the pile of letters and cards. Some from America, from France and Italy and even one from Iceland. She picked out the ones addressed in handwriting that she recognised and left the formal typed envelopes to await the secretary who came in daily to deal with them. She propped the large envelope with the crest on the back up by the leather ring case for later, and turned to the rest.

Carol wrote most days with amusing snippets about the dogs and the village and had come to see her twice, but her obvious grief was too much for either of them to enjoy the contact, so she wrote and sent love and Catrina absorbed her caring.

"If only," she'd said many times as if that was any use. If only was no help at all. If only I hadn't gone to visit Carol and if only she hadn't gone away leaving me alone to rest, was what she meant, Catrina realised. What could

Carol have done if she'd stayed? If only Paul had stayed with the sergeant in the cottage; two men could have overpowered even a man with a knife and a mad gleam in his eyes and prevented tragedy, but it had happened, and everyone had to face it.

Carol wrote, 'Paul rang.' Catrina tensed. 'He rings most days now that he's back in England and Ireland but he can't as yet get to see you.'

Catrina recalled the horrified face bending over her as they wrapped her in soaking blankets to dowse the fire. It must have seemed to him like the woman in a book she had read years ago, when a woman of great beauty shrivelled before a man's eyes as she became the age she really was, two thousand or so years old.

She touched the edge of the dressing on her face. Her cheeks were thinner today after the swelling had gone down, and after the last irrigation far less stiff, but she no longer demanded a mirror. That could wait until she was really used to the idea that Paul was repelled and now was haunted by the sudden loss of her beauty.

'Please come to me as soon as you can,' begged Carol. 'That is, if you can bear to see this place again. This time I promise you peace and quiet, and the garden is lovely just now.'

Catrina sank back on the pillows and considered. I can go to Carol and be cossetted, stay in a stately home, relax on a luxury yacht or go to Symfony, bless her, who would drive me completely mad in half a day.

I could go away alone to somewhere where I am not known or recognised, and come to terms with the blank looks and indifference that must be my fate in the future.

If it is any worse than my dear doctor says, I have to get used to people glancing and then turning away quickly. Carol's cottage would be best at first as the trauma would be less among a few people who might look, but not turn away, out of friendship for Carol, and might even be kind; somewhere safe away from official engagements and reporters.

So Paul was back again after another visit to the States and to Ireland. There were different ways of saying goodbye and he had done none of them. Was it goodbye to ring Carol to enquire but not to ring her or to suggest another visit? He's afraid that his eyes will give him away, she thought. His eyes were expressive and she could imagine them like the white flecked blue water of a mill stream that comes cold and uncertain over rocks, becoming grey. He could never hide his feelings and I would be lost for ever, she thought.

The junior nurse tapped on the door and came into the room. She was smiling. "Could you see a special visitor?"

"That depends on how special and who it is," Catrina said.

"Sergeant Richmond."

"Sergeant Gerald? Don't keep him in the corridor. Wheel him in!"

The electric wheelchair came smartly to the side of her bed and stopped. "Hello," Gerald Richmond said, and grinned. He took her hand and saw the worry stone. "Good. I wondered if it might be useful. I had it when I tore a tendon last year and it did more to rehabilitate it than anything. It's rather like chewing gum. Once you start, you can't leave it alone."

She warmed to him as to no other person since the accident. He hadn't said she looked odd, he hadn't made any comment about her condition and he just seemed very pleased to be with her. "How are you?" she asked. "You've beaten me to a wheelchair; that is, if you call that vehicle a wheelchair. It looks fit for the motorway! Nobody offered me a ride. I can go to the loo alone now but I can't stay out of bed for too long. I shall make them get me one of those and I can terrorise everyone in the corridors."

"You have to walk," he said. "Not much wrong with your legs." He came as close as he could. "You're thinner," he said. "Could have done with a less well-covered dame when you sat on my leg," he added.

"I don't eat a lot. Sitting in bed or in that rather nasty chair takes away the appetite." She laughed softly. "Detective Sergeant Gerald Richmond with a punk hair cut! It looks as if you chopped it with garden shears."

"Watch it," he said. "Your hair isn't so hot from what I can see. Why not have it all shaved off and wear a wig until it grows? You must have worn many wigs for your work, so why not now? What's different?"

Her heart beat faster. He had made no attempt to say what the staff would call the right thing. He didn't seem to mind that her hair was still ragged with charred ends, and that he couldn't see her face. "That's an idea," she said. "Sym wants to visit and I could ask her to bring something." She put a hand to the side of her head that had been badly burned. The skin was tight but it no longer gave her any pain. "I could tolerate a wig now."

"You haven't seen your friend?"

"Sym? Not the last time, as I was asleep, but she's coming back soon."

"Really asleep or faking?"

"Really asleep," she lied, and saw his disbelief.

"And the others?"

"What others?"

"Come off it. The scent of flowers swept the hospital. You've had the world and his wife enquiring and sending flowers and gifts and you say, what others!"

"People send flowers to funerals," she said, and his sudden anger sobered her. "I had a ring," she said more quietly, and opened the small case.

He whistled softly and held it to the light. "Never seen the Hope diamond before."

"Not quite, but it's pretty."

"A family heirloom or from Fifth Avenue or Mayfair?"

"You are much too subtle, Sergeant. Not Fifth Avenue; more likely Bond Street, on his way to his club."

"So it's to be the life of a socialite from now on? Lucky girl. Where do you go first? The Bahamas? Australia? Or the Scottish seat?"

She took the ring and put it away in the case. "Do I have to decide yet?"

"You should, if only to put the poor sod out of his misery." He glanced at her with searching eyes. "Don't tell me you're trying to convince yourself that he might be just doing the honorable thing by insisting that he still wants you? Join the bloody martyrs!"

"I love you," she said. "Nobody is as rude to me as you are. Of course he loves me. This would be a very expensive gesture if he didn't."

"Lots of people love you. If I wasn't spoken for, I'd be drooling there, first in the queue."

"Even with scars?" Her eyes were full of pain but he managed to show unconcern and didn't look away. "Even if I was so ugly that I frightened the horses?"

He gulped. "You may have scars on your face and body, Catrina, but you can't help that. If I'd been that much quicker . . ." Suddenly, his face was contorted.

"NO! I would have died if you hadn't saved me. Never blame yourself for that. You were wonderful, even if you can't cook. No, Gerald, I've come to terms with my vanity but underneath, I know I've changed. Some scars aren't on view and may never heal even if my face gets better. People I thought loved me may desert me now and then the hidden scars will deepen." She looked at the small leather case. "He loves me because I make him laugh and I wear clothes well. I could do that even with scars but if people like me only for my looks, I'm about to lose a lot of friends."

"Not the ones who count."

"Correction. One who counts."

"Where is he? He has been in touch?"

"He enquires and Carol keeps him informed but he wants out, Gerald. I saw his face when I came out of the van. I know that he has rejected me."

"I saw your face, too, remember. I don't suppose I looked exactly enthusiastic. You were a bloody mess," he said bluntly. "Bits of glass sticking out all over and blood everywhere, your hair on fire and your clothes burning. Not the moment to say I love you, was it?"

"Don't. You are a brute, Sergeant." She paused. "Did

it really look like that? Poor Paul, he would hate that. No wonder he keeps away."

"I came, but I had less to lose by seeing you again and it may stop me dreaming of you as you looked then. It could help him, too. He wants you. You do know that?"

"Paul has wanted me ever since we were teenagers but on his terms. Since he came back, he's wanted Catrina and all that she could do for him, but not Catty."

"You don't believe that."

"I didn't, but I do now." She sat straighter and looked beyond him at the bank of flowers. "Still they come and I have no idea who half of them are sent by. At least Catrina has given pleasure to a lot of people in the past and I can now retire gracefully. I was getting stale and wanted a change, so Max will have to look out for another talent and make another star. It will give him something to do."

"Shattered, was he?"

"Because I'm like this or because I can't work?" She shrugged. "I'm being unfair. Max came to see me and was very sweet. He is also genuinely upset about the girl who was killed. It's ironic. Patricia was the one girl he ever loved and she's gone." She thought of his eyes, still full of disbelief that Max, the man who fixed everything, couldn't fix death. "He says that he has a few up-and-coming girls in mind but he wants me back." She frowned and found that her skin could take it. "He seems to think I can work again. Do you think he's just being stubborn and refuses to admit to another defeat? Maybe his brain refuses to register that I can never appear in public as a top model as once I did."

"You'll work. There are other things. You said something about design. What could be better? If you hadn't been injured, you would have modelled for a few more years and then gone on to design or owning a business. It happened sooner, that's all." He pushed away from the bed and made the chair circle the pattern on the carpet. The wheels slid softly over the floor. "You aren't ill now," he said accusingly. "You are hiding."

"I'm not!" She felt her pulse rising. "I'm still far from well. I have no idea when I'll be out of bed for good and some of my skin is very tender."

"Accepted. But you aren't seriously ill. Feed up and put on some weight and do as the physio tells you."

"She's been sneaking!"

"Of course. We did talk about you," he said without guilt. "You could do better." He grinned. "A bit of an Amazon, isn't she? But good."

"What's the point?"

He wheeled the chair back to the bed and glared at her. "What's the point, she says! Do you think I like being in this bloody chair? Do you think I liked being strung up on a beam? Do you think I enjoy it when Wanda comes to see me and vows that she will never have another child while I am in the Force?" He cleared his throat. "I could have left you to barbecue in that van if I didn't think you worth saving, and you say what's the point!"

"I'm sorry. Oh, you know I didn't mean that. I owe my life to you and . . . oh, you terrible, lovely man, I hate you!"

He looked at her with tenderness. "Made you good and mad? Right. Your turn to visit me tomorrow, and stop playing silly buggers." He rang the bell for the nurse to open the door and Catrina waved goodbye, speechlessly.

Fresh blood seemed to run in her veins and she tried one of the exercises that the physio had tried to teach her. It hurt but she did it again and then once more. She was walking round the bed, holding on to the bed and chair and then the side table when Sym walked in. "Should you be doing that?"

"Yes. I've been given a lecture that I'm skiving. Sit down, Sym, and thank you for coming. Tell me all the dirt." Sym's eyes widened. "Yes, I'm better and I want to know what's going on out there in the real world, if you can call your set-up the real world."

"Paul's been to see you!"

"Who is Paul?"

"Well, someone has livened you up a bit. Not Paul?"

"Paul doesn't come to see me, but I have other friends who manage to bully me. How is the show shaping?" She took the marble egg and played with it, her hands more supple than a week ago.

Sym went into details and it was good to listen and not be directly involved. It didn't matter any more. From time to time Catrina made a remark or a suggestion and Sym made a note of a few things. "Can I come back tomorrow with the sketches and talk some more?" she asked.

"Not tomorrow. I think they're taking out another chunk of glass in the morning. The last piece with any luck, or so they say to make me submit to it, and then they can sew the bit up to fit the rest of the road map and leave it to get better, to get worse or just sit there." It mattered far less now and even the thought of renewed pain held no terrors. "Ring tomorrow and they'll tell you when you may come and I'll make sure you get priority among my visitors. How's Louis?"

"Need you ask?" Sym's hands spread and her eyes looked at the ceiling. "I'll kill that boyfriend. Twice he's gone to Brighton with a rent boy and put Louis off his stroke. He also gets up the girls' noses telling them how marvellous you are and how he wishes you were back again." Sym put a box on the table and looked embarrassed.

"Not another present?"

"Look, duckie, it's not my business, as you know, and I never interfere."

"But you feel you must?"

"You know the people who brought out the Orchid Look?" Catrina nodded, and hoped that Wanda had got her make-up for her birthday. She made a mental note to give Gerald the full range that she had been given by the firm on the day it was introduced to the public. "Well," Sym said, still looking as if she wished she had never mentioned it, "they also do a range of masking cosmetics. You might like to try them for a time after the dressings are off and the skin is whole."

"Sym, you are an angel! I would never have thought of that!"

"How soon can you try it?"

"Not yet. The last piece of glass is the worst, I think, and other bits are still oozing. I can't expect a miracle, but if it's possible, with make-up, to walk among normal people again, I'll try it. It would make all the difference. I'll feel human!"

"And come back to us, duckie." Sym looked triumphant. "Don't put on weight, duckie. The new range is for
the waif look. That silly cow who did Peter Pan has a lot to
answer for. Everyone is doing the gamine little-boy-lost
look and I've done a honey of a design for you."

"You never give up, do you?" She leaned back, her
eyes pricking with tears. "Get out, you scheming old bag,
and let me rest."

Sym chuckled and helped herself to all the white lilac
on her way out. "Don't give the best of the roses away,"
she said. "I'll be back for some more."

The rest of the personal letters had to be opened. One
was from the earl, anxious for her answer and making her
want to cry. He's too nice to keep waiting, she decided,
but I have to see my face first and then I'll ring him.

One letter had an American postmark and was dated a
week earlier. Her heart beat faster. Paul had come back
quicker than the letter, but he still hadn't come to see her.
Carol would be home now in the cottage and may have
seen him, she thought, and pushed the unopened envelope
away. She reached for the telephone but the monotonous
ringing depressed her. Carol should be there when she
needed her.

The letter had to be faced. She slit the end and smoothed
out the letter. Paul wanted to marry her however much she
was disfigured. He didn't put it quite as baldly, but that
was the message she registered. He was prepared to stand
by his proposal of marriage and hoped that she would feel
well enough to have him visit her soon. It had been written
all that distance away in America. Perhaps from a distance
she was less real and from the frantic backdrop of the Big

Apple, he could face his own sacrifice through a haze of Bourbon.

She tore the letter into shreds and began on her exercises again, ready to show the world that Catrina had not disappeared into the flames. She tried on the ring and ate some salad, the last meal before her operation tomorrow, in case she needed more than a local anaesthetic.

Paul's guilt was so obvious and so unnecessary. Who was he fooling? She knew what his feelings were and it would be better for him as well as for her if they called it a day and he slipped out of her life as he had done once before. It was the young Paul she now recalled, with the shadow of the complete man less important behind him in her mind. That Paul had been clear-cut in all his desires, his decisions and his beliefs. He was selfish but loving and very young.

Had success and experience made the Paul who avoided her less honest? She tried to get Carol again but with no success. But Paul had asked her to marry him, even if that offer was now heavy with guilt, offering something false. So where was love and real caring?

Nurses came on softly placed feet and Max telephoned late enough to make Sister frown, but Catrina insisted on taking his call. "Sym's been on the blower," he said. "She thinks you're much better and will soon be back in circulation. That's really great."

"You sound more cheerful. It can't be only for me."

"Yeah, well, we have to keep going, but I'm a bit weary."

"Why not take that break you were going to have? You need it and must be able to spare a few days."

"I might run down to Cannes. It's time I did a talent spotting tour of the bars and hotels," he said without enthusiasm, and Catrina sensed that he lacked the lascivious anticipation that he usually showed before such trips. Poor Max, this might even be a genuine business trip.

He asked her advice about something trivial but it pleased her. Sym wanted her back, and Max was prepared to wait for her and to help her in every way possible and not to ditch her as he had done to others, so he must think her return was possible.

The young doctor came to take her blood pressure and go over her chest, avoiding the tender spots where glass had recently been embedded. "The last theatre visit," he said cheerfully and noticed that she wasn't worried. He glanced at her chart. "No tranquillisers? Good. See you early tomorrow. Sleep well."

The nurse took away her water flask and gave her a mild sedative and the girl who had once been Catrina, world famous model and fashion queen, curled up in the foetal position, feeling like Catty again.

She couldn't believe her own awareness of what was going on around her. She had even managed to think about the security of the valuable ring and it now sat in the office safe with her own less precious jewellery. The ring was still impersonal, like borrowed jewels for camera shots, and as yet raised no pride of possession.

Once, she had worn a ring that had made her finger greeny-black, a ring from a Christmas cracker. Or had it been given her? She smiled sleepily. Forward little bitch. She had told people that Paul had given it to her and he had not denied it when teased by his friends. Her

175

left hand began to ache and it wasn't the contracted skin that troubled her. In time it will be better and able to take a heavy ring, she decided. I shall add a plain gold ring and keep them for ever. But as usual, she couldn't picture a future with Julian or any other man.

The sedative wafted gentle clouds about her and her sleep was light and good. Fear no longer had a place in her room and she felt warm. Dear Sergeant Gerald. She dreamed of his wife, heavily pregnant, and then remembered what he had said in anger. A trolley came in through the wide open doorway and she woke with the dream still inside her. Wanda had told him that he must leave the Force or she would never have another child. The first had been conceived with passion, unplanned and outside the regularity of marriage. Did passion die and give way to moral blackmail? The sergeant could never be anything but a policeman, and hadn't he once said that his wife had been a WPC?

The coloured antiseptic was cold on her face and the ache went deep into the hollow made by the glass splinter. If Wanda felt so deeply and was really frightened, then the gift of a wide range of expensive make-up might be taken as an insult, an unspoken effort to mask the lines that had nothing to do with complexion, a mental pat on the head and the dangling of pretty things to take her mind off the possible loss of a husband.

I'll ask the sergeant to tell me when the heat is off, she decided, and then I'll send it to amuse her. Even if she throws it out, she'll know I'm grateful.

The trolley was cool under the white cotton gown, and the blanket warm and light and red, like a fever victim going to a Victorian isolation hospital, she thought. The smell of the preparation made her think of dentists, but her teeth were still perfect. Her lips, too. She ran a dry tongue over them. That injection of course, and no way of drinking even an ounce of mineral water. She closed her eyes, promising herself a litre or two as soon as it was allowed.

It was so easy to be in the hands of impersonal and efficient people. Would marriage to Julian be like that? From the ornate vestments and fine candled altar would she be led away and told what to do and be moulded into a life that was not hers? He loves me, she told herself firmly, as another smell took over, making her senses dull. Paul was a million miles away and would be for ever.

Nine

"You must be out of your mind." Sym was already selecting the flowers she wanted to take away with her and she had only been in the room five minutes. "Sure you don't mind?" She took a spray of orchids and chuckled when she read the card attached. "Labour MPs now, is it? He's got a hope! And he'd have a stroke if he knew I nicked his orchids."

"I'm quite sane. I have a right to refuse an offer of marriage if I want to." Catrina sat in a chair by the window and looked out.

"He's the catch of the century and nice with it. I still think you're out of your tiny mind." Sym glanced at the woman who sat with a silk scarf half hiding her face and neck and a blonde wig concealing the newly-healed wounds on her scalp. The face was quite good and in time there was no reason to suppose that the once beautiful woman would not be acceptable again in the fashion world, but it would take a hell of a time. "How long now since the accident?" she asked.

"Months, years, who knows?" said Catrina and smiled, but without the joyous gift of humour and generosity that had marked her as someone apart from the studied loveliness of most models. No longer would her natural effervescence have to be damped down before she could project the haughty and detached expression that was needed for some creations. She'd be good but not sensational. Sym picked out some roses flown in from Cannes with the dew on them. "I lost track of time after the accident," Catrina said.

"Have you actually told him?"

"No. I want to see him first. I haven't let him see me since the dressings came off and I was sure that the last operation was over. They have done everything possible now and I must wait for any improvement that may come later as the deeper tissues heal and the blood supply improves." She laughed without humour. "Max says I'm mad, too. He thinks I should keep at least one string and that one ought to be the most profitable. Julian does have a lot to offer."

"You refused Paul, too?"

"That was no true offer. I wrote to him as soon as I received his letter. It must have been a welcome let out. I haven't heard since and Carol is very cagey about him."

That had hurt. She had been so sure that he was offering to keep to his proposal of marriage even though she had never accepted it, partly for the love he had once had for her as well as for conscience. Once they had loved each other when they were supple in mind and spirit and could see the future with clear eyes. No letter, no phone call and only vague news of him from Carol, who seemed too embarrassed to mention him. It was a relief to know he was back in the States.

Sym looked like a punk bride, holding flowers under

her chin and unaware that pollen from a lily was dropping over her blusher. "He'll not take no for an answer easily. He'll want you as soon as he sees you. Seriously, you have nothing to worry about as far as looks go now. True, you'll need the masking make-up for a while and you won't be able to caper about the platform so much for sports wear, but the rest will be easy. How's the leg, by the way?"

"Better, but you have to face the fact that I shall never do bare leg modelling, Sym, so don't get carried away. If you want me for the rest, I can do it once I get used to the stares again."

"You must come back. We need you. Don't give the earl the elbow yet. Once you are in circulation again you will live life on your own terms and you may find that he is what you need as a background and for security."

"He says that he can wait." Catrina picked up her worry stone, which had been with her since Sergeant Richmond gave it to her. "I'll have to wait and see how much he flinches when he sees me again."

"That doesn't mean you sit there with no make-up and no wig and an expression of dying duck!"

"Don't scold me, Sym. Don't you think he ought to see what he'd get when I'm ready for bed?" She smiled with more amusement than before. "What a pity I haven't a wooden leg to unscrew." The heavy marble was cool and like a friend. The tendons on her arms and hands were back to normal, the only trace of injury being a shiny patch on one palm and an ache when she was tired. She looked about her at the attractive hospital room. "They say I can go out of here tomorrow for good, and not just for a break before the next op.

It's strange. I've been out three times but always came back here."

"And now?"

"I'm not sure. I think it's back to Carol." Catrina bit her lip. "Even that might be the last time. Carol marries her big-wig in a few weeks' time."

"Why not buy the cottage?"

"I had thought of that."

"So you haven't given up all idea of being hostess of a great house but you need to have your own small pad?"

"Something like that." But it wasn't. Catrina couldn't admit her dread of losing Carol and the memories of the cottage, with pictures of her childhood and of Paul. Better to make a clean break and maybe buy another cottage in a location where she could be free of the past.

"You could never feel secure there," Sym said. "The accident would be on your mind whenever you locked the door and were alone. Marry your earl, honey, and at least you'd never sleep alone again at night, or if he was away you'd have staff on call."

"It's an idea." But Sym couldn't tell if the idea was for the earl or the cottage. "I have to wait for a final examination by a dermatologist who will tell me if the new skin can take make-up and I'll let you know what they say. The appointment is later today, so I shall stay here until then."

"I shall expect you at the salon in two weeks' time. I have the series almost complete and I've earmarked four fantastic dresses for you and some jackets and trousers that will take you straight back into Vogue."

"They haven't used up all the old ones yet. How they

181

keep using the old commercials puzzles me. I thought that I'd be forgotten within weeks, but Max had so many things salted away that didn't even depend on high fashion that Catrina goes on and on, and all our usual sponsors remain happy."

"The fashion scene is the reason why you have to appear soon. We aren't exactly ready for golden oldies and nostalgic back-glimpses of fashion and we've used the summer and autumn ones, taken six months before they were needed, thank God. The winter catalogues were out early but now we need something new." She laughed. "Max doesn't miss a trick. Summer in Oz being six months away from ours meant that he sold a lot to them for later and they'll never know the difference."

"So you don't need me. You can invent veils again and use girls muffled up in tweeds or masses of misty tulle, or have that ghastly white make-up again." She shivered. "No, never that."

"Don't be difficult. You can walk well now and we need you. You have to appear soon, Catrina, for all our sakes. The new series will be just right for you and anyone who knows very little about the accident will think you've been on a health farm slimming to prepare for it." She looked at the delicate shoulders that were slight but well formed, with an undertone of fragility just right for the new clothes, and the narrow hips essential to the boyish Peter Pan look. "From my point of view, you couldn't look better. If you put on a pound of flesh I shall be very annoyed, and the hollow orphan eyes are fabulous."

"I didn't do all this just for you, Sym!"

"A pity. It would make good copy." Sym laughed,

pleased that her own hunch had come off so well and more delighted than she'd admit that the woman who had given so much to the salon and to her was recovering not only physically but mentally and spiritually. She sat on the bed, scattering pollen everywhere. "You have to appear soon. Murmurs are coming out in the Press that you are disfigured for life. Unless they see you, they will write all sorts of lies and use the work in the can as proof that you are doing nothing fresh." She snorted with disgust. "One little bimbo even asked if you wore an iron mask."

"Don't! I still dream of the weeks when my face was completely covered, and the dressings stuck and had to be irrigated away. I know I'm very lucky." She looked up, the wide eyes huge in the fined-down face. "You think they might write that sort of thing now?"

"If you don't appear. You have been so famous that your fans must wonder and Max has been as close as an oyster. There have been whispers and enquiries from every country where your pictures appeared, and even a few from Eastern Europe and Asia. If such far-away places are curious then think how Berlin and Paris and London are seething for news."

"They would soon get tired of speculation," Catrina said.

"You can't afford to wait much longer. You could develop into a James Dean figure which would be death to your reappearance. The Press would want you dead or the professional equivalent. Much more profitable for them to use your old pictures already filed and keep the new Catrina off the front pages, having had to pay for the new stuff! Do you want a profession or a shrine?"

"It couldn't happen. I'm still alive!"

"Glad to hear it. At times you could have fooled me." Sym helped herself to a chocolate from an open box. "I'll take these too. You can't eat things like that!"

"How very public-spirited! They only happen to be from Floris! From an Italian Count."

"Not your type, ducky, and these are very fattening." Sym wrapped them in some tissue paper and popped them into her huge bag.

"Anything more? Grapes, petits fours or sugared almonds?"

"You can have the grapes and almonds. Ooh, lovely. What masses of all my favourites."

"You can leave that lot. I'm taking the rest to Carol. You aren't the only gutsy female I know." She glanced at the clock. "I wish he'd come and give me the go-ahead. Surely the last X-ray can't show any more glass. Only a precaution, he said, but he seemed to want another picture."

Her hand trembled. The last session had been the worst, with more pain than she'd anticipated, and she wondered if she could take any more. The euphoria given her by drugs and a basic fatalism had given way to pain and new discomfort where the new grafts had been applied and from the aggressive assault to perfectly good skin when they took the last graft material from her other thigh. This time, with a clear brain she realised that if the surgical procedures failed, she was doomed to a degree of permanent mutilation, and she wanted to live. How she wanted to live now and walk in crowds and under the trees! But she doubted if she had any reserves of courage left.

If the X-ray showed nothing, then it would be goodbye to this place, and the future would depend on her own resilience and the wonder of natural healing.

"I have to go." Sym bent to kiss her.

"Going hospital visiting?" Catrina asked. "You leave here with far more than you bring." She laughed. "Give my love to Louis and tell him I wear his turban when the wig gets too hot and it's absolutely dreamy."

"I'll tell him. Don't do anything rash. You could be very happy in idle luxury. Just give *me* the chance."

"You'd hate it. All those old horses braying in their tweeds and the others neighing in stalls close to the house. Too much fresh air for you, and rainy evenings playing bridge."

"I could bear that for a month, but don't be trying to tell me that Julian would make you do that. He's kindness itself."

"Goodbye, Sym, I'll be in touch." Sym was right. He was kind, but such kindness could be overpowering and difficult to take. Thoughtlessness and neglect could be fought but could she bear the weight of his goodness? As ever, when she was alone, the handsome aristocratic face was a blur in her mind. If he disappeared and she never saw him again, would she grieve? Could he ever leave an ache that was too deep for tears?

She opened a newspaper and saw the account of a business congress held to save a manufacturing company from Carey Street. Her eyes stopped, flickering away from the picture at the top of the page. She recognised one of the Americans who had been in the bar of the Ragged Bear the night she had dinner with Paul. On that night, Paul had said he had things to discuss with her and her limbs had softened with desire. If only . . . But she had said all her if onlys. The American was talking to the trade minister and his group of advisors. Another man stood with them. He was tall and very thin and surely the face, sideways to the camera, couldn't be Paul? Not Paul who was broad of shoulder and muscular to the right degree of solidity, but never thin as the boy Paul had been, thin and wiry and intense.

She clipped the picture out and put it as a bookmark in the book she was reading, deciding that Carol might like to see it. Had he been ill? Had this business crisis involved him so much that he worked twenty-four hours a day and had lost weight? She had been out of touch in a news limbo for so long that she didn't even know the significance of the meeting or the crisis. Was Paul losing a battle in his own trade? Could this be the reason why Carol no longer mentioned him as he was too proud to burden his friends with his worries?

Carol was a dear friend in whom he could have confided but might have chosen not to do so. But not me, she thought. He would never confide in her now, even if they kept a tenuous friendship without passion. Paul would hate to be less than he had been in her eyes. Losses of money and prestige would make him assume that she despised him as much as he despised her for her loss of beauty. He couldn't know that she could be beautiful again with the help of a little camouflage.

She smiled wryly. I can't blame him, she thought. He saw me covered with blood and with glass shredding my face; flames consuming my hair and clothes. He saw me again here, my face shrouded in white with only drugged eyes showing, and he went away, the horror in his face as visible as it had been in his first reaction on the hillside by the cottage.

The doctors came and gave her the all clear, after probing each area that had been treated. The scars were almost painless now and the skin pliable, no weeping at the edges of grafts and the tiny marks of minute stitches were fading.

"Smile," the surgeon said and the muscles did all the right things, but the underlying sadness was there in the empty smile. He wondered how any man could resist her now, or even if she had been permanently scarred. And that she was not, he thought. She saw the masculine approval and felt a quickening of her pulse in reponse to admiration. It was slight and as he probed a tender nerve ending it was gone but she knew that she had the spark alive and well, the gift of making men want her.

"We checked your masking kit in the lab and it's first class," the dermatologist said. "Use it freely and it will help to keep the skin supple until the scars fade more. I shall expect a signed photograph of the restored Catrina."

"I shall scatter them like confetti," she said and laughed with relief. No more ops and no more bed rest, just an injection of courage, please, doctor, she wanted to say.

"Stay tonight and leave in the morning," he suggested. "I expect you'll have a few calls to make, things to arrange. What are your plans?"

"I shall order my car to be here early and drive down to my aunt at her cottage before lunch, but I do have a visitor coming here this afternoon, so I shall be glad to stay for another night."

Once, she had said she owed nothing to anyone, but now she knew better. Max had been kind and affectionate, like a brother who really cared. That had touched her more than all the flowers and fruit and she had held his hand while he told her that Patricia had been the girl he wanted to marry, his first genuine love.

Sym had been human as she never appeared behind the catwalks and in the dressing rooms. Her habitual obscenities were mere punctuation marks that were purified in the hospital atmosphere and by her concern. They were the faithful, with Carol and one or two close old friends.

Catrina braced herself for the next visitor, and when he arrived, she sat by the window wearing no make-up and a slightly defensive expression.

"My dear little girl," Justin said. "You need feeding up, but you are very lovely." He smiled and kissed her cheek. "Why did you tell me that you were ugly?" His eyes saw what he wanted to see and would always see, and she could no longer bear it. How could she live with this dazzling and pure devotion? She burst into tears and he comforted her, puzzled by the outburst but firmly refusing the return of the ring. "Later, we'll talk about that. If it troubles you, just keep it and wear it as a gift from a devoted friend, but never give back anything that I want you to have. If, as you say, you can't marry me, then please let's be friends. Come away for a holiday and perhaps you may change your mind."

He left and she knew that he was only half convinced that she was serious. To a man who could demand anything wherever he went, what was one hysterical interview with a sick woman?

She shrugged and dried her eyes. It was comforting to have him in the background and she needed time. The make-up box was very comprehensive and she doodled with some of the items, rehearsing colours for the next day when she would emerge alone and not hidden in a closed ambulance car. As she worked on her face Catrina emerged as she had been known and she sighed. It opened some doors and shut others. She had the choice of anonymity and a life of idleness with Julian or a new fame. "Come in," she called when someone tapped on the door.

"Christ!"

"No, just Catrina," she said. "What happened to crime that you can spare the tax payers time to see me?"

"I heard you were back for final checks," said Sergeant Richmond. "I thought I'd look in."

"Quite the real detective," she said. "We shall have to stop meeting like this, Sergeant, darling."

He grinned. "We shall if you look like that. I think I was safer when you had that dressing on your face."

"I thought you loved me for my mind."

"A man can have his little fantasies even if Wanda would kill me if she knew." But his eyes were friendly and warm and they sat and smiled at each other.

"She must be relieved to have you back again. You look fairly normal. Even the hair has grown again."

He bent the finger that had been broken. "Funny, that. This gave me more trouble than the leg but it's fine now. I nearly asked you for my worry stone back again."

"You can't have it. I shall keep it always."

"Thank you," he said, quietly. "If I have to get hurt again, I'd rather be with you than anyone I know."

"Is that a compliment?" she asked shakily

"A big one." He grinned. "How is everything I can't see? Everything in working order? All ready for St Margaret's Westminster, or wherever?"

"You passed him on the way here?"

"Thought it was his car. It's routine to notice."

"You never miss much."

"No. Seen the news?"

"Just a glance." He saw the torn newspaper and didn't pick it up. "Are you back at work full time?" she asked. "Any trouble at home over staying in the Force?"

"Not a lot. A little coolness but Wanda has got over her panic, or at least, she seems better." He frowned.

"Does she mind you visiting me? I *am* the cause of your trouble."

"No, she's always been a fan of yours and she asked me to thank you for the make-up. She was thrilled to bits. She doesn't resent you. She has enough sense to know that if it hadn't been you, it could have been a similar circumstance that got me into that situation. No, she likes you and by next week, she'll have set up a salon at home, practising on all the neighbours. No, this other thing, her saying that she refuses to have more children, is from way back. Since Kim was born, she no longer thinks like a WPC and sees only the dangers and the threat to them both."

"Children make one vulnerable," she agreed, and thought, if I had a child, I would hug it against the world and protect the life responsible for its birth. If I had Paul's child, all skinny knees and tender eyes . . . she gulped. "Children must be hell," she said.

"And heaven," he said. "Wanda doesn't believe that I have the same feelings. Kim needs a brother or a sister. She's far too cute for her own good and needs the steam taken out of her."

"Wanda really means what she says?"

"We both mean what we say, so it's back to the Pill." He laughed. "What would I do if I left the Force?"

"Be my bodyguard if I marry."

"You haven't decided!"

"Quick as a flash, aren't you, Sergeant? No, I tried to give back the ring but he cunningly left it as a gift, and with it a sense of obligation. We are good friends and he wants to take me sailing."

"And Paul?"

"Don't be nosy, Sergeant Richmond. Paul doesn't come into this at all."

"When do you leave here?"

"I drive down to the cottage tomorrow morning alone. Not far, I know, but for me, an adventure, hence the try-out of war paint."

"Take care. I haven't time to spend on you now."

"Kiss me, Sergeant." He bent to kiss her on the lips. "Not too gooey?" she asked. He grinned and kissed her again.

"Flavour of the month. Goodbye, Catrina. It's been nice knowing you . . . I think."

She smiled long after he had gone, noticing that he had left the room with her lipstick firmly on his mouth. So, a man could kiss her without flinching and she could still bring a look to his eyes.

The loose top that Sym had brought her and insisted was for wearing at the cottage was filmy and yet a complete cover for her arms, and the matching harem pants did nothing to hide the shape of her legs but made the scars invisible. The weather was warm and she knew that she would need fresh clothes to fit her body and her situation. She rang Sym and asked for copies of the outfit in less expensive material. "And make Max pay for them. It's time I stopped accepting things even if I pay you with expensive orchids and chocolates."

"I ate the lot," said Sym. "So you've decided that Catrina has a future?"

"My face didn't frighten the Sergeant and the doctor had a twinkle in his eyes."

"And what about you-know-who?"

"Won't take no for certain but wants to be friends whatever I decide. That was with no make-up. He didn't seem to notice anything but said I needed feeding up as I was thin."

"So I can depend on you to come next week to try the clothes?"

"Yes." Catrina took a deep breath. She had said it and now there was no going back. One word to Sym was enough to bind her to a bargain.

"Good girl. Ten sharp and don't be late. Come in the back way. We haven't time for you to hold a bloody court, so play it cool." The old Symfony, sodding old pro, thought Catrina affectionately.

"You'll send the clothes down to the cottage?"

"They are on the way; in two colours and soft cotton. Two for the price of one, if you like. Knew you'd want them." The phone went dead before she could thank her and there was nothing now to do but pack and leave more flowers for the wards. She collected the pile of cards and put them in her case. People didn't forget, or some didn't.

The ring was in its case in her handbag, already an embarrassment with its size and value unless she wore it. It could get lost if she opened her bag in a hurry. She took it out, watched the evening light glint on the perfect stones and slipped it on the ring finger of her right hand. He said to keep it. She took a deep breath. It would be a talisman while she drove the car, a sign that one man loved her, scars and all. It sat comfortably on her right hand and she wore it in bed that night and until she left in the morning.

Gloves were awkward over rings so she discarded them. In warm weather they would look odd anyway and were no longer necessary. One more minor exposure to the air was good, and to curious eyes the shiny hand was flexible and only a close stare would make the scar obvious to strangers. One day, I'll swim again and sunbathe, she thought, but not today. The drive was test enough of her recovery and she wondered how she would feel when she reached the traffic lights where Giorgio had turned and she had seen the leg and foot of the dead girl in the back of his estate car. This drive was not nearly as far as the one from her apartment and she had no need to face the hassle of cars in the West End of London.

The road was fairly busy, busy enough to make her concentrate on her driving as she reached the dual carriageway leading to the familiar village. Masses of summer flowers made suburban gardens erupt with colour and the trees cast sweeping shade across the grass verges. She switched on the radio and changed from programme to programme in search of music that was neither too highbrow nor too shattering. Poetry for ten minutes was a pleasant and soothing balm and some Chopin filled a gap announced by an apologetic announcer who must have thought that nobody liked nocturnes in the morning.

Then came the news. The American Trade Delegation was leaving Britain, early in the day from Heathrow, and saying nice things about their visit that could mean anything or nothing. Catrina smiled at the hackneyed phrases of goodwill and wondered if the language was as flattering when they left in Concorde to report back to their lords in New York and told them exactly what had been said or agreed.

She glanced in her rear-view mirror as the lights changed. Since the day when she had driven with Paul, she noticed traffic lights and was amazed to find how many there were along this route. Music came back and with it tunes that had been period pieces before the Beatles.

It was soothing and she let it flow over her. She looked in the mirror and saw the car again. She was sure it was the same car, with nothing special about it; just a blue car with a sliding roof that sent shafts of light down onto the driver but hid him from her vision.

The Americans had gone back and she assumed that

Paul had gone back with them. No mention had been made of names in the news broadcast and she would have to look at television if she was that interested to know where Paul might be. She glanced back again. Why think of Paul now? The man in the car wore dark glasses and a cap that peaked over his brow. One good jaw-line could be any man. The ring twisted on the too thin finger and she adjusted it as if guilty to be wearing it.

The road to the cottage had been resurfaced since it was chopped up by police vehicles that had stormed up and parked in every corner of the lane and driveway when the van on the hill burst into flames. After that the lane had been full of television vans and news teams, all lusting after news of Catrina and details of where she had stayed, who with, what she had for breakfast and was she dead?

Even now, the hill gave her a cold frisson when she looked up at the top, and she was glad to see that the old shed where Giorgio had hidden the car was no longer there. A walk with the dogs might help to exorcise it all and would be another step back to normal. The music changed and she stopped the car in front of the cottage. She paused before turning off the engine and the music. 'Got to have a walking talking living doll,' she heard. She noticed a car door slam but it meant nothing as she sat listening to the song. She looked up at the hill and turned off the music. "Goodbye, Patricia, goodbye, Giorgio." He was surely mad and for him she had no hate now. Goodbye to all that had happened on that day so long ago.

"Goodbye, Paul," she whispered and transferred the ring to the other hand. It was over; the pain and the waste of emotion and time. Everything had to stop and everything must be forgotten or used. There was a parcel in the porch with the distinctive colours of Sym's salon on the label. The new clothes would be just as suitable on the yacht as they were in London or the village. Clever Sym.

Ten

She left the car and searched in her purse for the key to the cottage as there was silence after she rang the bell. Typical for Carol to be out with the dogs at the moment she arrived, Catrina thought. She smiled as she unlocked the door. It was good to be neglected. One more sign that she was human again and there was no need to handle her as if she might break.

The shabby hall carpet was stained as if Carol had not had time to clean up after the dogs' muddy feet, but the flowers on the table were fresh and welcoming. Everything in the cottage was comfortable without pretension. It was chintzy, but honestly so, as loose covers were the only practical solution in such a household. The brass was genuinely old and not tarted up replicas for the flea market, and the flowers were from the garden, smelling of summer as none of the hot house orchids had done.

The outer door opened again. "Carol? I'm here." Catrina called. "Shall I put the kettle on for coffee?"

"Enough for three." She swung round. "Carol is coming up the lane now. I'll get the cups," Paul said, as if they had been in the cottage together for hours and had never really been far away.

"Did you follow me?"

He flung his cap into a corner and smoothed back his hair. "If you mean was I travelling in the same direction, then yes, I was following you. Carol invited me here for the day and after stewing in London in the heat, I gladly accepted."

"I see." She went into the kitchen and heard him talking to Carol. The kettle overflowed under the tap and she tipped out the excess water. The gas lighter was sluggish so she used her own cigarette lighter and stood back, watching the dull metal of the kettle as the water began to sing.

Carol was a cow! Carol was one stupid bitch who had no idea of the effect that Paul had on her arriving as he had, out of nowhere. What did she think could be gained by such a transparent effort to get them together? It was obvious that he had no warning of her visit and must be as angry as she was.

He hadn't come for the cups, so that meant he didn't want to face her. Carol was a right cow! Anger heightened her colour but it was hidden by the thick masking cream. Her eyes, however, showed her emotion. She spooned instant coffee into three mugs and added boiling water, then filled a jug with more coffee. Paul hated instant coffee. Let him filter his own, she thought savagely. She added sugar to Carol's and Paul's and dashed in milk, leaving her own black as the discipline of work showed again. She ignored the biscuit tin and with perfect poise, carried the tray into the sitting room, the last of her limp now a sexy hesitation that she over-corrected to great effect.

The sapphires cut bright as a chalk blue butterfly as she
raised a hand to smooth back a wisp of hair under her wig
and Paul's hand stopped half-way to his coffee mug.

"How did it go?" Carol asked anxiously. Her eyes took
in every detail of the concealing clothes, the wig and the
make-up. "You look absolutely marvellous."

"I think I drove well. No nerves on the way here. I
saw the doctors yesterday before I packed and I don't see
anyone again except for a check in six months."

"So you aren't tied to one place?" Paul regarded
her with something akin to hostility behind the polite
question.

"No, I can join a party in Antibes if I'm back for my
check in time. I can go anywhere if it doesn't upset Sym's
plans and if Max approves. He was talking of Oz but I
don't want to do that just now." She looked at Carol,
hoping that she would help her out. "I can come here to
Carol if she'll have me or I can go back to my London
apartment and vegetate there."

"You could go to America."

She shrugged. "If that's what I wanted to do, but I have
no plans for crossing the pond."

"And life goes on as before?" His smile was bleak. "It's
good to see you looking so completely recovered and so
beautiful again."

Like hell he does! she thought. He is shocked! He's
shocked because I look as I do now and he hates it.
Why? Surely Paul can't be as low as that? It was one
thing to try to beat her at everything when they were
children together and it didn't matter, but now they were
two separate individuals with their own careers and lives,

with no need for sibling rivalry, no need to succeed at the expense of the other and no time to be childish. The ring slipped round her finger and she straightened it.

"Catty! You didn't tell me!" Carol blushed with surprised pleasure mixed with acute embarrassment. It had seemed a good idea when Paul telephoned to ask if he could come to her, and she took care to make it happen on the day that Catrina was expected. Rosy clouds hovering over her own coming marriage had obscured her good judgement. It would have been a fitting segment in her plans if Catty and Paul had fallen into each others' arms and rediscovered their love.

Sadly, one glance at them as they met in the sitting room, with the sunlight showing the magnificent ring to the frozen-faced man, killed all her hopes in that direction, but she smiled. If Catrina had decided to marry for affection, position and wealth, who was she to weep over lost memories? Paul had lost out and Julian had the prize. She took Catrina by the hand and the loose ring slipped off into her palm. "It's beautiful. I thought my ring was super but this puts it right out of the running." She put it on her own hand and made the stones throw fire.

Catrina was suddenly tired. She took her coffee to the windowseat and stared out across the garden and up the hill to the deeply-leaved copse and the waving grasses of the meadow below the rise. She sipped black coffee and retreated into mental abeyance, and Paul's shadow came closer.

"You really are going to marry him?"

"It looks like it," Carol said shortly. If Paul had been less unfeeling, the ring she now held need never have been placed on the finger of the woman he professed to love. His face was pale and Carol hated to see him suffering but she had seen that look before as he grew up, and he had only himself to blame. She put the ring on the sideboard and picked up her bag of groceries. "Chops all right for lunch?" she asked.

Neither of them answered her and she went into the kitchen and moved about noisily, opening and shutting cupboard doors. Catrina poured more coffee for herself but made no effort to re-fill Paul's mug and she walked back to her seat as if she was alone in the room.

He was angry with the deep cold anger she recalled from way back and she was devoid of feeling. She wondered if there would ever be a return of sensation. One of the dogs came and sat on her foot, quietly as if he knew that only in silence would he be tolerated.

The make-up began to feel warm and moist in the hot rays of sun through glass and when she touched her cheek, her finger came away stained. It was like this after a long session at a fashion show. She moved out of the sun and knew she must monitor the temperature of her surroundings when wearing the stuff.

"Excuse me," she said politely. "I have to unpack." Paul watched her go and she knew that he wished he had stayed in London or gone back to America with his friends. Carol put her head round the bedroom door and handed in the parcel from Sym. "I'm sorry," she began.

"Thanks for bringing that. I'd forgotten it," Catrina said. "Let me know if you want help with lunch," she added dismissively, and Carol escaped back to the kitchen.

The bedroom mirror was a good one, handed down to Carol by an aunt who had come from a very affluent and dignified background. The reflection was true and unyielding of flattery. Slowly, Catrina wiped away the thick creams and colours and yawned to stretch her face. It was good to be free of the muddy concoction and she cleansed the skin thoroughly and noted that the daily improvement continued. Each day she could put on less and less make-up and unless she was under bright lights for photography or at a show, she could use the lighter version that came with the collection of cosmetics. She patted skin food onto her cheeks and into the scar on her neck, which was still slightly tender. It was all responding in a way that a month ago had seemed impossible.

She took off the wig and shook out the short curls that now grew in baby fine tendrils over her ears, with a fair fuzz on top. The Peter Pan look again, she thought and smiled. Sym had been delighted when she saw it and now it would probably set a fashion to wreck the ideas of other fashion houses, taken for granted in the glossies. Sym would laugh all the way to the bank and Max would smile again.

She unpacked the rainbow turban and found that it matched the silky top and trousers. Cunning old devils. They would set two fashions going in one. She arranged it to hide the worst scar that couldn't as yet be hidden by her natural hair and felt light and clean again. Paul was no longer worth considering and if he objected to sitting at lunch with a woman wearing no make-up to hide the damage, then he could go to hell. If he could want her no longer when she had lost her gloss and the more vibrant facets to her personality, she didn't want to know. He had come back to the UK to make a claim on her and use her to further his own success, but the accident, the long silence and the Atlantic lay between them now, cold and impassable.

If he had stayed away, I could have yielded to Julian and to the life he offered with pleasure, and joined the lovely women who give new blood to the aristocracy. Too bad, Paul, she thought bitterly. You should have stayed away. You've ruined everything and you came back too late. If you had made love to me the night after we were at the Ragged Bear I would have said yes and perhaps this would never have happened. I'm on the 'if onlys' again, she thought.

It's better like this. I know about people now. My lovely sergeant is real and the life I may take is real, but placid, never reaching a climax of joy or a pit of despair. I shall be cradled in care and swamped by protection. While I am vulnerable to stares, I shall need Julian and his love, but what then?

She moved restlessly. This coming back to life was more painful than her wounds. Did flowers, pushing up between flagstones feel pain in their efforts to reach the air? Yet the tender shoots must have supernatural strength to get through the parched earth and to break the stones. My sap is rising again, she thought, and I must grow and spread myself into independence. The sensation of the silk on her skin and the expertly simple design was soothing and she remembered a design on which she had worked with Louis. If he used it, it would fit into the new series. She had an urge to telephone Sym and knew that she was still a professional.

A tap on the door made her turn sharply to the mirror to make sure that the turban was in place. "Sherry?" called Carol and when she went into the sitting room, Paul was pouring the pale Fino into exquisite glasses. "Do you like them? I love beautiful glass and Paul brought them for an engagement present. I shall expect the flutes and wine to match when I get married. He brought the sherry too as he remembered the supermarket stuff I usually buy."

"Very nice," Catrina said and raised her eyebrows when Paul put his glass down clumsily and it slipped off the tray, shattering into fragments.

"Oh, *no!*" Carol darted into the kitchen for dustpan and cloth and looked close to tears.

"Don't worry. Just as well it was me," Paul said. "I'll make sure you get another." Catrina sat still, staring at the broken glass, remembering the sound multiplied a thousand times and flames catching her hair. Paul took her glass from her hand and set it down carefully. "One was an accident, two would be ridiculous," he said. "Better break a couple of matches to make the three breakages, before anything serious happens. Are you all right?"

"Still a bit fragile," she said and drew away from him. His eyes seemed to magnify each scar on her face and she wished she had been less defiant and had covered them again. At least now you know how I really look, she thought. Now you can see why marriage with you would be impossible. If you looked at me with those grey-blue eyes, wanting the beauty that is lost and not really wanting the real me, I would die a little more each day.

She said nothing, but merely sat back in a chair and put a hand over her eyes as if dizzy, then smiled weakly. "Is the cottage still on the market?" she asked when she could breathe again. She looked at the deep windowseats, the beamed ceiling and the wide stone fireplace and wanted it as her refuge, cosier than a stately home, where she could hide if she found the world too pushy.

Carol blushed. "You said you didn't want it."

"Is it sold? You haven't finalised yet, have you?"

Carol glanced at Paul and sipped her drink. "She has sold it and it will be finalised," Paul said. "I bought it, as it is, except for anything personal that Carol wants to take away and couldn't live without."

"I thought you hated chintz," said Catrina, her anger stimulating her to not caring what she said. "I seem to recall a boy who couldn't wait to get away from cottages and villages and England."

"That was after you left."

"No, it wasn't. Even then you spent your time boring me with what *you* would do, all the triumphs in store for *you* and where *you* wanted to go. You had already left the country, in your mind."

"I wanted you to come with me." Carol murmured something about cauliflower and slipped away to the kitchen.

"To trail one step behind you and iron your shirts?"

"At first, maybe," he admitted. "But eventually you would have had everything that any sane and normal woman could want."

"Then I'm not sane! If that makes sanity then I'm as mad as a hatter. Not once did you listen to what I wanted to do with my future."

"It could have been *our* future."

"What if I'd said, come with me and build *my* career, *my* contacts and *my* life, which I will share with you, and even give you a public pat on the head when I've made it?" Her face was blotched pink and pale where the skin tightened unevenly and the blood supply was still poor. "Well, I didn't need you, which was just as well. Where were you, Paul? Where were you when I was living in a freezing bedsit and breaking my heart?"

Her tears fell, spotting the bright silk of the shirt and she knew that her face must be contorted and ugly with weeping. He turned away, his hands shaking. "You never broke your heart. You never needed anyone but Catrina."

"Oh, you call me Catrina now, do you? In the police station you did another vanishing act. Miss Milsom alleges that a crime has been committed. I didn't see it, officer, and I strongly suspect that it might be pre-menstrual tension, wink, wink." She dried her eyes and began to laugh. "Come in, Carol, before the chops are burned. I'm hungry and Paul and I have nothing more to say about us, so we'll be civilised and talk about the weather."

"Bitch," he said quietly and grinned. "You were good at that in the old days. The times I had to let you have the last word because you made it impossible for me to answer back were so many that I can't think how I ever forgot them."

Catrina smiled and went to help Carol, and when they

206

sat down they were perfectly polite luncheon guests, enjoying good home-cooked food and having nothing more important on their minds than the temperature of the Chablis. Catrina ate well and wondered if Sym would be horrified to know that she ate cheese and chocolate gateau as well as sauté potatoes. She stirred her black coffee when she was once again sitting in the windowseat. "What are your immediate plans, Carol?" she asked.

"Well, I hoped you might stay for a few days so I stocked the freezer. Do you mind if I slip away after tea? I promised I'd go to Michael's mother for a day to help her choose her wedding clothes. She's rather a pet, which is a great relief, and she's dying to meet you some day. You could come with me today. She'd be thrilled."

"Not today, but I assume I shall be invited to the wedding?"

"Of course. I can invite you now, but the cards will come later." She glanced at Paul and smiled.

"I might not be here," he said slowly. "I should have gone back today but I needed a few days to myself. There's a need for someone to divide his time between the States and Europe and I might opt for that. I just don't know where I shall be when you get married, Carol, but if it's possible to hop on a train or a plane, or a donkey, I'll make every effort. I have to talk to Sym again, too."

"Why Sym? I thought the chain store contract was done." Catrina resented him having any contact with her life, as if in some way he was even now cashing in on her success. If he had wanted her only for her face and figure, he could bloody well do without the brushed-off gilt of her reputation to further his trade connections.

"This is something more." He lit a slender cigar and she wondered how many other habits he had acquired since he left England. The solid gold watch and the silk shirt might be unremarkable on many men she knew, but to Catrina he was Paul, the boy with torn shorts or frayed jeans, with rough patches on his knees from scraping on the bark of trees, falling from his motorcycle or being dragged along the rugby field. This gloss was as unfamiliar to her as her sophistication must have surprised him when they met again in the fashion world. We are strangers now after all this time, who glimpsed each other for a moment and then lost touch again, she thought.

His eyes as he watched her on the catwalk had not watched Catty. The man she now saw, very assured, with the backing of wealth and success, was not the scatty kid she had loved. Now, she too had no hint of the past left. She was not the slim girl with the fresh face and budding body that he loved, so it was the end of two people, and their replacements didn't count.

"This is something different and I wanted to talk to you, too, Catrina. If we sign this new contract with Sym and Louis, they want you to work for us, too." She opened her mouth to speak but he put up a hand. "I know you aren't really fit yet but we can wait. We do want you and not some nameless girl with no professional background," he said.

"I come expensive," she said crisply. "It's something you'd have to discuss with Max and I am not prepared to work as hard as I did in the past, or under the same pressures."

He inclined his head. "We pay well and we think a

tomorrow I must phone Julian and make it for real, she decided. She tried to recall his gentleness and the wonder of his devotion but could think of nothing but the fine hairs on the back of a man's hands. What must she take with her when she went to Antibes with Julian? She would have to have more of the creations that Sym had designed for her, but now all she wanted to do was to change into loose linen trousers and a sweatshirt and walk to the top of the hill in moonlight.

Firmly, she turned her thoughts to her future. The flat in London must stay as a convenient pied-à-terre where she would be able to take Sym and her crowd and the often extrovert buyers and designers who she had to see and couldn't imagine receiving in the solid mansion overlooking the park.

Paul came back with coffee and found her nibbling one of the petits fours that she had brought for Carol. He took the box and helped himself. "Just in time. I see you've eaten most of the almond ones."

"Sorry," she said. "I didn't know you liked them. You would never eat marzipan chocolates when I knew you."

"I learned to love them."

"Did she leave them and eat all the hard centres?"

He grinned. "Something like that. It was enough to break up any liaison."

"Such a little thing." She looked away.

"The tip of the iceberg. The other reasons went deeper."

"She snored?" The lightness was getting brittle.

"No, I kept wondering if you did. I kept wondering if you'd changed, and each time I saw another perfect picture smiling up at me from a magazine, I wondered what went on behind that smile, in that lovely head."

"Not true, Paul. You were away for far too long to make me believe that." She remembered the silence, the empty evenings, the absence even of Christmas cards. "Confess," she said and tried to smile but the skin on her face was suddenly tight, as it had been between ops to remove the glass. "You forgot all about me until I was famous and you decided that you could use me. You came back to win my face. The other me wasn't important."

"I saw a picture of you when I was already quite well-heeled and it made me sad. I saw that you had everything you wanted from life, and it didn't include me." She stared at him. "I recalled the Catty I'd known and loved."

"And left."

"We parted. Neither of us left. We were impatient; jealous of each other's potential and frightened that we would never make our own individual fortunes." His face hardened. "And as you grew in beauty and fame, I knew it was too late to go to you and tell you I loved you. I know I was right. You would have laughed at me, believing that I wanted to take and not to give. I hated your beauty. I hated every perfect picture that haunted me wherever I went."

"But that was the reason why you came back; to use my beauty and professional reputation."

"I had to make one effort to win you even if you laughed at me and it killed my pride for ever."

Catrina looked at the one red bar and longed for a log fire. "I saw your face, Paul. It's no use pretending. I saw your face when they pulled me from the van, and you were horrified. You could see my beauty disappearing just as the doll was dissolving in the heat and you went away. You couldn't bear to see me disfigured. The woman you wanted had everything and you had prospered to match her success, so there would be no need for rivalry again if you married her, but the girl who looked as if she might have no face or future in our business filled you with fear and disgust."

She looked out through the uncurtained window to the hill and saw the rose-red sunset on a rock, setting it aflame.

"You're right," he said. "I was horrified. I was horrified to see you hurt. I wanted to fling myself on that madman and kill him with my bare hands but he was already beyond revenge or justice. They pulled me away and made me get into a police car." His voice was hoarse. "It's a wonder they didn't arrest me; I hit one of the officers in an effort to get at the man and then . . ."

"And then?"

"God help me, I was glad. I wanted to take on your suffering, but if you were disfigured you might need me at last. I was so shocked at my own thoughts that I couldn't bear you to see me. I couldn't face you in that hospital after the first visit as your eyes accused the world and I knew I was guilty of something I hoped you would never suspect. I felt like a hermit who needs to flagellate his body to save his soul, so I kept away even when I longed to be there with you. I tried to will you to get better and to have your beauty restored even if it meant I could never have you."

His face was thin and taut and the eyes beaten and

hurt. She saw the Paul she remembered and knew that he suffered. "And now?" she asked.

"I saw you today, risen again. Complete and needing nothing I could offer you." The effort to smile wasn't worth it. "Today I've had too many shocks. First you appeared as you had been, entirely beautiful, with a ring big enough to make an angel blink, and then you came in as you are under the make-up, and Carol is short of a beautiful glass."

"So now you know that it is all done by mirrors; an illusion that I can turn on at any time. Tricks and tinctures and skill make for miracles." Her smile was softer. "Some more scars will fade, Paul. Some will stay and a part of me will never be the same again, but I know now who are my true friends, I have my work and I have discovered that I can be alone and like it."

"And I have never loved you as much as I did when you came back to us, wearing no make-up but loads of pride and a touch of defiance."

"I have to begin somewhere, so why not with Carol and an old friend?"

"Does that mean you didn't care what I thought?"

"Yes. I have no time for people who pretend. I've found that life is shorter than I'd supposed. My friends must take me as I am."

"And lovers? A husband?"

Her smile had a roguish edge. "I've had my chances, kind sir."

"But you intended to live here alone, sometimes? Even if you marry a title?"

"It seems that I can't do that for much longer. I believe

the property has been sold, so I must cut my losses and look elsewhere."

"Only to a caretaker. I'd hoped to keep it warm for you."

"Do caretakers live on the premises?"

"Of course. They potter about the garden and cook and give devoted service at all times."

"In this small community? Aren't you afraid of the dreaded curtain twitchers?"

He appeared to be shocked. "Careful! The caretaker would have to be respectably married."

"Don't come here with your Middle West morality," she said and laughed. "I might hate you sometimes."

"I hope so. We could never live together without that sharp edge." He came closer and touched her hair. She froze and wondered how she had existed without that contact for so long.

He kissed the scar where the soft down grew over her ear and slipped the silk from her shoulders. The deep scar began to ache under his lips and her body roused from apathy to a slumbrous heavy lethargy that wanted to give and to give and live again, knowing that with Paul, she need never be anyone but Catty, the girl on the back of the bike, with the wind in her hair, and love making them cling together for ever.